PURPLE SHADOWS

Empty Colours: Book 1

D. T. Moorhouse

ISBN: 978-1-8380736-1-9

CONTENTS

PURPLE SHADOWS

D. T. Moorhouse

CHAPTER ONE

Michael Hill Memorial

I want to ask you to do something for me. Don't worry, it's nothing difficult. You can do it where you are right now. What it is, is to just use your imagination for a moment and picture in your mind a nondescript, ordinary old town. It might be like yours. Or it might not. That is up to you. It has a name but it doesn't really matter. Make one up if you like. There is a relatively small population in this town, though it is larger than some others I can think of. It is populated mostly by young people, not a lot of old ones. They don't wait long to have kids in this town. When you enter the town, the main street you first encounter runs like a vein right through the heart of the town, branching off in all different directions. To fields and parks, to housing estates, to derelict factories that were once the driving force of the town but are now just shadows of their former selves.

At the far end of this main street, standing solitary, looking over the town is a formidable, red brick building. This is the town's oldest and least popular secondary school. This is my school. Well, it is the the one I attend. Standing three storeys high and several hundred feet wide, it is flanked by huge wrought iron gates that are in dire need of painting. But considering the fact that they have been in such a state for as long as anyone around here has been alive, I seem to be the only one that takes any notice of that. On the wall above the main entrance to the school is a huge, faded sign that reads "Michael Hill Memorial Secondary School Est. 1854 by Sir William Hill in memory of his late father Sir Michael Hill". This inscription is followed by a short Latin phrase that is supposed to be the school's motto. They told us what it means on our first induction day here but I can't remember exactly what it is. Something to do with integrity, or intelligence. Something beginning with an I. But who cares, it's not really important. It is not like anyone around here abides by it anyway. But I'm rambling now, sorry, getting lost in my thoughts. Zoning out, sort of. I have started to do that a bit recently. Well, quite a lot actually, now that I think about it, but you will probably notice that yourself, if you can stick with me.

So, when you have an image of all that in your head, picture if you can, inside Michael Hill Memorial, a classroom. Completely ordinary, like any other. Where posters that try to promote 'Proper Learning' and encourage students to be "Learning Ready" adorn the paint chipped walls and hole filled noticeboards. Where desks are lined up single file. Where the tops of those desks are covered in almost indiscernible scribbles of insults and tags such as "Jonny suks cock" or "Kenzo woz ere 2k8". The sort of immature nonsense you would expect from the hordes of hormone ridden adolescents that pass through the classrooms every year. Where ,underneath the tables, dried chewing gum from at least twenty years ago has now made its home, waiting for an unsuspecting first year to reach under, touch it and stifle a shudder when they realise what it is they are touching.

At these desks sit the students. A mixture of gender, race, class and most importantly, intellectual ability. I don't know about the school or schools you attend or have attended but here at Michael Hill there is always a marked distinction between the intellectual levels of the students in any given class. In this school it is generally split into three different, distinct categories. These are, in no particular order other than the way they are coming to me: the top of the class, the back of the class and boths sides of the class, pressed up against the walls. There is also the middle of the room. But the middle of the room is a sort of no man's land. No one ever really ventures there. Those who do usually don't stay in school very long, either dropping out or transferring to a different one. How you perform academically will determine where in the room you will sit for the five or less years you attend the school.

The clever ones, the ones that do their homework every night and take part in the extracurricular activities, sit at the top of the class. These are the students that actually engage with the teachers. They are always the first ones to raise their hands when a question is asked, always the first to volunteer for any task. But most importantly they are the ones that the rest of the student cohort simply don't like. That's hard to imagine, right?

And that is where the students like Jack Hawkins sit. This guy, Jack, is the brightest kid in my year, probably even in the whole school, sitting smack dab in front all of the teacher's desks in every classroom. But, as clever as Jack Hawkins is, he is even more unpopular. Nobody really likes him. Except the teachers, they love him. But they would adore him, wouldn't they? The perfect, little, studious, goodie two shoes. A perfect punching bag for the bullies. Personally, I've never had a problem with Jack. I mean there is no reason why I should. Our paths rarely cross, apart from the odd nod of acknowledgement in the corridor. And the guy is just being himself, trying to actually do well in this crappy town.

At the back of the class is where the bullies sit. These students are otherwise known as The Dossers. Or The Messers. Or, to put it most bluntly, The Ones With No Ambition To Go Anywhere in Life. These are the students that everyone knows will end up either rotting away in prison or working in the local supermarket or fast food restaurant (not that there is anything wrong with working in those places. If that's what you're happy doing, then by all means go for it and make the most of it.)

Most of the time these are actually not bad kids, they have just had the crappiest of crappy upbringings, resulting in poor academic performance and in turn a lifetime spent bullying others. But there are a select few like Jimmy Browne, Carl Hopkins (Jimmy's second in command, who lives with his nose shoved so far up Jimmy's ass that I'm surprised it hasn't been stained a permanent brown colour) and the rest of their little gang, who live just to see other people suffer. These guys are the worst kind of student a school can ever have. They have no sort of moral compass at all. They will beat up a guy just to watch him squirm in pain. They are scum. Not that I would ever say that directly to them though. I like my teeth where they are.

Around the classroom a handful of desks will lie empty, their normal occupants no doubt truanting, or possibly down by the bike sheds puffing away or stuffing their fingers inside Jenny Crawley. But at either side of the classroom sit the most interesting people. These are the students that are stuck in a sort of limbo. They are clever enough, that if they applied themselves just a little more they could be sitting at the top of the class. But they don't want to be seen as geeks, outcasts, nerds. They are also popular enough to be sitting at the back with The Messers. But as much as they don't want to be seen as the swots they are equally reluctant to be seen as out and out wasters. So they opt for the middle ground, the limbo, at an equal distance from each group, never fully reaching their potential, never fully stooping to the levels inhabited by the bullies.

These students who inhabit the sides of the classroom are the ones that the teachers, especially the ones who actually seem to care, like Miss Perkins for example, who teaches English, try their hardest with. These are the ones that teachers know they can make a real difference with. Sometimes they succeed in converting a side of the class student to a top of the class student but cases like these are very rare and often take a special kind of teacher to make that happen. Often their attempts mean that these students are regretfully sometimes pushed further backwards, condemning them to a life at the back of the class. But most of the time they remain stationary, spending their lives as 'Side of the Classers'.

And that is where I sit. Yep, that's right. Me. Dean Turner. Seventeen years of age, devilishly handsome, mightily funny and an eternal 'Side of the Classer'. Forever stuck in limbo. Forever rejecting every attempt of teachers like Miss Perkins to convert me to a front of the class student, while never fully accepting the offer from the wasters to join their unruly ranks at the back of the room. And to be totally honest with you, I am actually happy here. I am comfortable with being a 'Side of the Classer', content with being just your average, everyday kid. I don't want any extravagance in my life. I am happy to just be as normal as possible. But one thing I would like to think about myself is that I am one of the good guys. Pretty level headed, pretty cool, the kind of person people find it easy to get along with.

And sure, I make my fair share of mistakes, without ever getting involved in anything too serious, but what teenager doesn't? I work just enough to get decent grades without ever excelling myself, while at the same time doing enough to remain relatively popular so that the scum at the back of the class don't use me as target practice for their wayward fists. And like I said, I'm happy. I am genuinely happy just being a good, normal guy.

And I suppose this is the point at which I will begin documenting my story, so to speak. I mean it is as good a place as any, right? You know a little about me. I have established who I am (finally), you know what school I atttend, you know what type of person I try to be. So I suppose I should just dive right in. But, I should probably mention that I'm not great at this sort of stuff, expressing feelings and thoughts and stuff. I might not always get things right (though hopefully I won't get things horrendously wrong either). And I might not always be such a fountain of knowledge. So please, just bear with me. And if I start zoning out a little, just go with it, I usually get back on track fairly quickly.

CHAPTER TWO

Friendly Fire

Monday. 9:15am. The start of the second week of a new school year. Double English with Miss Perkins. It is only fifteen minutes into the double class and it is already starting to bore me to death. I mean come on people, who in their right mind would put double English on a Monday morning? Are they seriously trying to kill us? I suspect they are. Trying to whittle us down slowly over time. I can even see the headline of the local newspaper now "Group of students found dead at Micheal Hill Memorial School- Cause of death: Boredom!"

I would be much better equipped to deal with Mr. Shakespeare and company after a lengthy lunch. Don't get me wrong though, I like English. I do. It is one of my favourite subjects (not that there are many of those to begin with). But I definitely cannot be dealing with it first thing on a Monday morning. That is just pure torture. My brain, although physically in my head, is mentally still back in bed on Sunday. It won't be awake for, I would say, at least another two hours. And to make matters even worse the class is taught by Miss Perkins. She is a perfectly adequate teacher and any other time I am perfectly happy to be taught by her. But I would rather not be in her company on a Monday morning. (Sorry Miss Perkins! It's nothing personal really. I mean, I do have my reasons, but I'd just rather keep those reasons to myself!)

But I must say, as bad as I make it out to be, I am thankful that it's not double History with the dreadfully dull and brilliantly boring Mr. Usher. There would definitely be a mass extinction in the school if that were to happen. And I don't think the school would like that much bad press. It's bad enough as it is anyway. I'm not slating the school when I say that, it is just that the school already has a bit of a bad reputation. And it's not really the fault any particular students or teachers per se. It has just always had a bad reputation for as long as anyone around here can remember. I think it stems from a couple of incidents back in the eighties. (But don't quote me on that!)

Since then people just stopped sending their kids to the school, afraid of how it might affect their future career paths I assume. Not that many kids show a lot of promise around here anyway. There are usually just a couple of dozen students in each year, and there were as few as only fourteen students in my brother Darren's entire year when he attended here. But, to be fair, it has been slowly and steadily making its way back up the ladder. It is not perfect and not nearly as good as it needs to be. Yet. But there is still hope. I wouldn't write it off just yet. Especially if they keep getting students like Jack Hawkins to enroll.

Jack is in my year. He is in most of the classes I'm in. English, Biology, French, Geography -just most of the usual ones. But he's a top of the class student, so he does extra subjects, like Music Studies and Economics, all the ones reserved for the smartest kids in the school. I bet you have probably already heard that everyone hates

Jack (It is pretty common knowledge in the school) but that is not strictly true. Now, I'm not about to say that that is a lie and, surprise, Jack is actually really popular and I'm just saying that because I have a problem with him. No. That is not the case. He's not popular. Like at all. I have seen him talk to maybe one or two people in the whole four years I've been at this school with him. To be honest the kid is every bully's wet dream. From the way he dresses to the way he talks, he is just asking for it. I mean he has an LGBT support badge pinned to his schoolbag. That is just a big no-no in this school. Come to think of it, why has he even stayed here for four years if his life is so miserable? He must be crazy. Or putting himself through some sort of rigorous mental training.

But yeah, the bit about not absolutely everyone hating Jack. That would be me. I don't hate Jack, not by any means. I don't particularly like him, he's just not the sort of person I would hang out with, but I certainly don't hate him. Mainly I just feel sorry for the kid. He is just being himself and gets picked on for it? Constantly. Like, I'm talking hourly here. In the corridors, in classrooms when teachers backs are turned. (Note to self: be a bit nicer to Jack, even if it is just to say 'Hey' when passing, the kid needs it.)

But what kind of a fucked up school is that though, eh? Jesus, what kind of fucked up world is that, where a person can't even be themselves without enticing hatred from people that haven't even spent enough time in their company to form an opinion? I seriously worry for the future of humanity sometimes. And they talk about colonising other planets in the near future? I think they should worry about fixing the mess they've left this planet in first, before jetting off to others. And that's coming from an eternal 'Side of the Classer' like myself. Jesus, we really are fucked!

After English it is Maths with Miss Constance. Not a lot happens here. Pretty mundane stuff. Lots of quadratic equations and Pythagorean theorems. Hours of endless fun! NOT! Miss Constance is most definitely the strictest teacher in the school. Eyes like a hawk, on the front and back of her head! Her strict nature has even earned her the nickname 'Corporal Constance'. So no shenanigans ever happen in her class. There was one incident though. Last year. Pretty crazy stuff. But I'm afraid I can't talk about that. We're not allowed to. No, seriously we're not. The Board of Management for the school made the whole class sign a non-disclosure agreement. And I am not breaking that. Not even for you. I'd rather not face those repercussions, thank you very much.

But finally, after Corporal Constance's intense Maths drills, it is time for lunch. Hallelujah! This is definitely the part of the school day I live for. Not for the food. I could do without that stinky cafeteria rubbish. No, what I like best about lunch is that I get to be with my two best friends and Karen. Wait, have I not mentioned Karen? Crap, don't tell her that. Karen Shelley, (considered by most of the horny teenage guys around here as one of the most attractive girls at Michael Hill Memorial) is my girlfriend. We have been together, officially, for about seven months, texting for about two months prior to that. Yeah that's right. We started texting just before Christmas and got together officially on Valentines Day, believe it or not. She is my first proper girlfriend. Well one that's lasted for more than a week or two anyway.

But things between us have not been going so well recently. In the beginning everything was great, we were all over each other. Well, it was really Karen that was all over me. But lately things have been a bit weird. Karen hasn't been herself for a couple of weeks. She has been kind of distant, not really texting as much as she used to. But I think sometimes that maybe the problem is me. Maybe I just haven't been spending enough time with her. Maybe I'm the one that's being distant. I mean I'm happy and all that I have a girlfriend but I'm just not really *into* *her* if you know what I mean. And it's really only because of my friend Dave that we got together in the first place. He knew her first and introduced us. He is the one that encouraged me to get with her even when I wasn't so sure.

Anyway, we are sitting beside each other, eating lunch, chatting. I spot Karen raise her eyebrow and smile to someone over my shoulder. In less than one tenth of a second later I feel something collide with the back of my head, sending it forward, knocking the chip I was about to put into my mouth out of my hand. It lands halfway across the table and I twist around to see two guys standing about ten feet away, bent double, clutching their sides with laughter. I look on the ground to see what hit my head and spot, of course, a dildo. A pink dildo. (Yes, you read that right, a pink fucking dildo! You couldn't make this stuff up!) But I would expect nothing less from those two idiots.

I pick it up and examine it while the two guys start making their way over to us, noticing how real it looks, the length, the girth, the veins running up the shaft, how strange, yet comfortable, it feels in my hand. When they sit down opposite myself and Karen, I toss the sex toy across the table to the taller of the two guys.

"Grow up, you two."

"Don't be so serious Turner," he says, catching it in his

right hand.

The two idiots that have joined us are Dave Rudden and Luke Hughes. My two best friends in the entire world. I have known Dave since we were four. He is the very first kid I met on my very first day of school. Our mums always like to remind us of that day any time they see us together. Apparently, we took a shine to each other immediately and had become friends in the schoolyard before even entering the school. And the worst part (according to our overly doting mothers, who may or may not be exaggerating) is that we held hands going into the classroom and did so every day for the rest of the school year.

Why do mums always like to bring up the embarrassing moments from their children's lives? We were four years old for God's sake. Get over it. It's not like we are still doing it. Not that it's going to make any difference to them though. I can see mine giving the speech at my 50th birthday party, telling everyone how her little boy loved his friend so much that he just had to hold on to him. Pass me the sick bucket, please!

As for how Luke became our friend, I can honestly say I have absolutely no idea. I don't think Dave does either. We hadn't met him until we started Micheal Hill Memorial and he just seemed to be there one day, chatting and then never left us alone. He sort of just integrated himself into our lives from day one. But as it turned out, he is a really great guy. So we invited him into the fold. He's funny, tall, broad shouldered and incredibly handsome. (I sometimes even find myself staring at him, thinking about how goodlooking he is. But don't tell anyone I said that.) He is the perfect ladies man. And boy does he let you know it too. Never stops bragging about how many girls he's been messing around with.

"You're lucky Corporal Constance isn't on lunch duty today," Karen says to them. She points to the sex toy that is resting on the table in front of Dave. "She sees you with that stupid thing and you'll be expelled for sure."

"Where did you even get that?" I ask, eyeing the dildo as Dave is stuffing it into the front compartment of his schoolbag, the shape of it somewhat discernable through the fabric.

"It's a long story," he says back to me, his eyes looking not at me, but over my left shoulder. "I'll tell you all about it some time, but that time is not now Turner, for I have just spotted my next potential victim."

CHAPTER THREE

Dave's Mistake

We all follow his eyeline across the packed cafeteria and spot Jack Hawkins leaving through the double doors. Before any of us can say something to stop him, Dave is on his feet, following Jack out into the corridor. Crap! Please do no do this today Dave. Don't be that guy. I give Luke and Karen a look that says 'let me handle this' and head out after my friend, ready to put a stop to whatever is about to happen. Because I know if anyone can talk Dave out of being a complete asshole, it's me. I know him better than I know myself. But that's what happens when you spend every day with a person for the past thirteen years (except Christmas and major holidays obviously).

He's not usually an asshole though, to be fair to him. He is usually a pretty good guy. There is just something about Jack Hawkins that seems to have rubbed him up the wrong way. Maybe he just likes to pick on Jack because everyone else does. Maybe he just doesn't want to become the target of Jimmy Browne and his stupid little gang, so he asserts his dominance over the weaker members of the school. Not that he gets much of a chance to do shit like that. I always try to steer him clear of doing anything really stupid or doing any real harm to people.

But it's been getting much harder to do lately. And I could tell from the look in his eyes as they followed Jack across the cafeteria that this will probably be the hardest one yet to stop. I hurry along after him, trying to call him back without raising my voice too much. I don't want to attract the attention of any teachers who may be wandering about on lunch duty.

"Dave. Stop. What are you playing at? Leave him alone."

"Leave off Turner, I'm just gonna have a bit of fun."

"Yeah but at whose expense Dave?" I ask in a raised whisper. "Weren't you saying just the other day how you hate bullies? How is this any different? This school doesn't need another Jimmy Browne."

I catch up with him and grab him by the crook of his elbow. He jerks his arm away and turns to face me. I see Jack over his shoulder turning right, into the boys bathroom, oblivious to us behind him. As he turns, the LGBT support badge pinned to his schoolbag reflects the sun that is beaming in through the window at the end of the corridor. At least he is out of harms way. For now. Looking up into Dave's face, I see a look I have never seen on it before. There's something wrong. He seems angry. I give him a light punch on the arm.

"What's up with you?"

"Nothing."

"Don't try that crap with me," I say. "I've known you for thirteen years. There is definitely something wrong with you. I can tell. Spill."

"I said there's nothing wrong."

"Is everything alright at home? Your dad?"

"My dad's fine."

"Then what the fuck is wrong with you?"

"Nothing."

"Alright. Fine. Don't tell me, but don't fucking say I didn't try to help. Ungrateful shit." I look at my watch. We still have twenty minutes left of lunch.

"Come on, stud," I say to him. "We still have some time left."

I flash a cheesiest of cheesy smiles across to him which he returns reluctantly and we start making our way back to the cafeteria, back to Karen and Luke, but the noise of a door opening behind us makes Dave stop and look over his shoulder. So I look back too. Bollocks! Of course it is. Perfect bloody timing! Why couldn't he have stayed in there for just a few more seconds?

And which way does he turn to walk?. Yep, you guessed it. Right towards us. Dave stops in his tracks and crosses his arms as he leans against the wall with his schoolbag, a sinister look on his face. I lean up against the opposite wall, facing Dave, watching him, trying to pre-empt the attack I know is coming, so I can intervene in time.

I leave my hands by my side, instead of shoving them into my pockets like I usually do. Jack walks towards us, smiles at me, nods his head and passes right between us. Dave just watches him pass. Phew! I thought I was going to have to go all fighter mode on Dave but it looks like he's letting whatever was grinding on him earlier slide. I relax my shoulders for a second but tense them back up again when Jack is only a step or two ahead of us and I hear Dave say:

"Oi Hawkins, I found something that I know you will just love."

Before I can comprehend what the hell is happening, Dave's right hand is in the large compartment in the front of his bag and he has grabbed Jack by the front of his shirt. Like lightning he has pulled out the dildo from earlier is trying to shove it in Jack's face.

"For fuck's sake Dave, STOP!" I shout at him, probably a litte too loud.

Jack looks absolutely horrified and tries to pull himself away but Dave's grip is too tight on his shirt. I lunge forward and try to swipe it from his hand but Dave ploughs his shoulder into me and I'm flung sideways into the wall. Disorientated for a few seconds I hear Jack begin to cry and beg Dave to stop. This needs to end. Now. Before someone sees. So I straighten myself up and, forgetting that Dave is my oldest and best friend, I curl my fingers into the palm of my hand and plunge my fist straight into his jaw. It knocks him sideways and he lets go of Jack's shirt.

"Go. Don't just stand there. Run!" I yell at Jack, grabbing the dildo out of Dave's hand, now starting to feel pain ripple through my knuckles.

He turns and starts to run and Dave who looks at me in complete shock, his hand now holding the side of his face. Giving him a thoroughly disapproving look, you know just in case the punch wasn't enough to show how pissed I am at him, I turn and run in the same direction as the fleeing Jack. I try to catch up with him but he is running too fast. I need to apologise. But more importantly I need get him to stay quiet. For all our sakes.

"Jack, wait, I'm sorry."

He slows down and comes to a stop when he hears the sincerity in my voice. He looks at me, frowning.

"I thought you were coming to-"

"Ha, no I was just-"

"Oh My Goodness! Is that?- No! How. Dare. You. Bring.

Such. Filth. Into. This. School!"

My eyebrows meet just above my nose. Filth? Oh crap! I realise I still have the dildo clutched in my hand. I look down at it then up at Jack. He looks just as terrified as I feel, his eyes wide, his lip trembling slightly. Hurried footsteps approach us and I can hear the disgust in Miss Dolan's voice when she reaches us and speaks again.

"Do you think it is funny to bring this atrocity into school? Do you?"

"No Miss, It's not- I mean- please just let me ex-"

"Enough!," she says, silencing me with a *very* curt wave of her hand. "We shall see what Mister Danvers has to say about this behaviour. Absolutely disgusting! Follow me now. Both of you."

She marches us through the corridors, me still clutching the dildo in my right hand, Jack looking like he is about to pass out. I try to give him a reassuring look, but it probably comes across more scornful than anything else. It feels like we are being led to our execution, Miss Dolan, the guard, escorting us to face the firing squad, while Jack and I are the inmates, resigned to our solemn fate.

She continues to stomp ahead of us in silence until we get to the principal's office, where she walks straight by the secretary, opens the door forcefully and gestures for us to enter. Mister Danvers, sitting in his plush, leather chair, looks up from his computer when we enter. A look of shock, followed swiftly by one of confusion crosses his face when he sees who has just interrupted his lunch break and what is taking uo residence in my hand. Miss Dolan heads straight for his desk, bends forward slightly and talks in a hurried whisper while myself and Jack stand just inside of the still open door, the secretary behind us craning her neck to get a better look at the action. When they're finished, Miss Dolan hurries past us and shuts the door, but not before letting us know, by way of a horrified facial expression and a loud tutting noise, how disgusted she is. Danvers doesn't invite us to take a seat, like he usually does when you are summoned to his office. Instead he walks around and stands in front of his desk, his hands twisting around each other, palm over knuckle. He doesn't speak for a moment, probably trying to decide which words are most appropriate to use in the situation, what to say that will be least embarrassing for us all. Eventually he reaches over and takes the dildo from me, with his index finger and thumb, creating a pincer grip and places it gently on top of his desk, as if it is a live grenade.

"Would either of you care to explain what this abomination is doing on school property?" He gestures to the toy lying on his desk. "What possessed you to bring such a thing onto these grounds? Miss Dolan says she found you brandishing it about, outside the Art classroom. What was it you were intending to do exactly? Hm"

I stay silent, thinking hard, feeling the awkwardness growing between the three of us stood here. I can't hand Dave in. Even after what he just did. He is still my friend after all (Well I hope. I mean I did punch him pretty hard). He wouldn't grass me up either, I'm sure of it. So I say nothing, choosing instead to continue staring at at the office floor. I expect that Jack will tell Danvers everything that happened. He will land us in it for sure.

I sneak a glance sideways but see that Jack has his head bent forward staring at the ground as intently as I am, hands interlocked in front of him. He must sense that I'm looking at him because he gives the slightest shake of his head. An indication that he's not going to blab. Thank fuck for that! He is probably too embarrassed to say anything. I know I certainly would be if I was him. After a few more moments of silence from both of us, Mr Danvers speaks again.

"Fine. If neither of you are willing to talk, then I see it only fit that you both receive two weeks worth of detention and a letter *will* be sent home to your parents. That should teach you some respect. This is a very serious matter. And have it be known, even the slightest breach of any more rules will result in your immediate expulsion. Do I make myself perfectly clear? Well, do I?"

We both nod our heads.

"Right then, Both of you are to report to Room B17 after the last class today for this afternoon's detention, and you will do so each day after that for the next two weeks. Now get out of my sight immediately."

CHAPTER FOUR

Detention

Monday. 4:15pm. And I am still at school. Nope, there is no need to got back over that again. Your eyes have not deceived you. It is correct. I am still at school. On a Monday! At 4:15pm! Forty five minutes after I should have been whizzing through the front gates, hopping on the bus and making my way back home. I am living in an actual nightmare! And it is all thanks to Dave bloody Rudden. The idiot landed me in detention. Two poxy weeks worth of it! And all for trying to protect stupid Jack Hawkins. Well that is the last time I will be doing that, I can tell you. The little tosser can defend himself from now on. Even from Dave.

He keeps trying to make eye contact with me from across the room. (Yeah that's right, Jack is also in detention because of Dave.) But I keep my head down, pretending to write. I'd rather not let him see how angry I am. Two completely innocent people gone down for crimes committed by Dave. Just you wait until I get my hands on him. The fucker needs strangling!

But is it my own fault? Should I just have let Dave pick on Jack? Maybe. I'd be at home now if I had. But I couldn't do that. I'm not that kind of person. I'm better than that.

Besides, I can't let my friends turn into complete ass-holes. And I cannot let them pick on people who have done nothing but be themselves. I would be just as bad as Jimmy Browne and his gang of bullies if I let that happen. No, it was right thing to do. Definitely. It is just unfortunate I ended up here. In prison. Well no of course it's not prison, that is clearly an exaggeration, but it might as well be. Especially since Corporal Constance is in charge of today's detention.

I mean this is just turning out to be the worst day ever. First, my lunch with my friends is cut short, then I have to stop my friend bullying an innocent kid, then I get nabbed with that stupid fucking thing in my hand. The only way this day can get any worse is if I go home and find out the house has burned to the ground with my family inside. Anger is making me exaggerate now but still, it's a pretty bad day. By anyone's standards.

The Corporal wanders around the class every ten minutes, looking in to everyone's notepads. A look of approval here, a snort of derision there. I finished pretending to write ages ago and now just have my head resting in my arms, eyes closed, thinking about what other fucked up things are going to happen to me today.

I must have been drifting off to sleep because when I open my eyes and look up again, everyone is gone, except for Miss Constance who is sitting, straight backed with folded arms, at the desk at the front of the room, looking across at me, a smug look across her wrinkled face.

"No, no, you take your time there, Mr. Turner. It must have been a very taxing day for you."

"Oh absolutely Miss, worked my poor little fingers to the bone today. Just needed a quick pick me up."

I suppress an immediate groan, realising what a stupid

mistake I have just made as I wouldn't normally answer back, especially to Corporal Constance, but I have had just about enough of today.

"Oh, is that right young man? Well, you will just have to work them a little harder tonight to complete a one thousand word essay on, let's say, rather aptly, The Merits of Sleep, due at the beginning of tomorrow's detention."

"Miss, please, you can't be seri-"

She stands up, her two hands placed flat on the table in front of her, leaning forward slightly, her nostrils beginning to flare.

"Shall I make it two thousand Mr. Turner?"

"No." I clamp my teeth down on the sides of my tongue, to stop myself from saying anything else stupid.

"Good. Now leave. I don't know about you, but I would like to get home some time today."

Not wanting to spend another minute in school or risk getting any more punishment work, I gather my things, stuff them into my bag and throw it onto my shoulder. I sprint out the door, down the stairs, through the corridors and out into the fresh air. Stopping at the bottom of the concrete steps to take a deep breath in, I look down at my watch. It reads 5:07pm. Fan-fucking-tastic! It will be well after six o'clock by the time I get home now.

I run my hand through my hair and decide if I should walk or get the bus. If I walk, I can take the shortcut through the old distillery but run the risk of running into Jimmy Browne (he likes to hang out around there with his scumbag mates) or I can wait for the bus, probably get stuck beside some drunk guy or drugged up yob who will either try to sell me weed or ask if I'm selling any. And considering the day I have already had, I am definitely not in the mood for that right now. Besides I get on okay-ish with Jimmy Browne (at least enough for him to refrain from turning my face into a bloody canvas) so it looks like my decision has been made. I walk out through the big, wrought iron gates and trun right but stop, my foot hovering in the air, when I hear someone calling my name from behind.

"Dean, hey Dean, hang on!"

I turn around and see, running towards me from the other side of the street, none other than Jack bloody Hawkins. What the hell is he doing here? Did he wait for me? I think about just walking on but, bearing in mind what Dave did to him today, I willl give the kid the benefit of the doubt. He didn't grass us up after all so, for that at least, he deserves some respect.

"Hey Jack, what's up?" I say to him, nodding in acknowledgement when he catches up with me.

"Oh, er, nothing, I just waited for you over by the bus stop, because I know you usually get the bus home but I saw you turning this way. Are you not heading home? I thought you would have been with it being so late?"

"Yeah I am, I just feel like walking home. That okay with you?"

"No, yeah of course, I didn't mean- sorry." He lapses into silence and looks at me all awkward so I widen my eyes and raise my eyebrows to get him to continue talking. "Mind if I walk with you? I only live a couple streets away from you. And I hate getting the bus anyway. It's always full of drunk guys and, er, one time a guy tried to sell me drugs."

"Um, yeah, sure, I suppose."

So, it's not just me that notices that about the buses. That is actually a bit of a relief if I'm being honest. I was thinking I look super dodgy or something. We walk in awkward silence for a while, Jack opening and closing his mouth every few minutes, as if he is going to say something but decides against it. He probably wants to talk about what happened earlier but doesn't know how to bring it up. Poor kid. Always so awkward.

"So you said you were waiting for me at the bus stop? I ask him, trying to break the awkward silence in the hopes it wull spur him on to say whatever it is he wants to get off his chest.

"Yeah, I was. I, er, just wanted to say thanks, for, er, what you did earlier, I know that Dave guy is a good friend of yours. It was brave of you to punch him like that. It mustn't have been easy, you know..."

He stops talking when he sees me narrow my eyes at him. He looks really nervous. We turn left at the end of the street, the old distillery looming ahead of us in the distance.

"Don't worry about it. No need to thank me. I was just doing the right thing. Anyone else would have done the same if they were in my shoes."

"I wish that were true," he whispers, more to himself than to me.

We walk in silence again until we reach the gates of the distillery. It was once a thriving factory, the most successful in town but it was closed down about seven years ago. About 150 jobs were lost when it did. My dad's being one of them. Now it sits alone, bleak and abandoned. Just a shell, a memory of a once thriving business. We squeeze through the opening in the fence at the left hand side and walk around by the imposing building.

"I just wanted to say sorry aswell."

Wait, what? I'm confused now. Sorry? What is he sorry for? What the hell has he gone and done? Shit! Has he got older brothers, cousins? Is he leading me into some sort of ambush? Please, God, if you are real, do not let my final moments on this planet be here, alone, in the grounds of an abandoned factory with Jack Hawkins. Surely I deserve better than that. I look around at my surroundings, all of my senses now on edge, expecting someone to jump out and attack me at any moment.

"Sorry? What are you sorry for? You didn't do anything wrong?" My voice sounds high, shaky.

"No, I know that," he says, looking at me with soft eyes. "But if it wasn't for me, you wouldn't have ended up in detention. If I wasn't the way I am, then people wouldn't pick on me, Dave wouldn't have done what he did and you wouldn't have gotten the blame for bringing that, er, dildo thing into school."

There are tears beginning to form in the corners of his eye, a strain evident in his face that was absent a moment ago. He is obviously trying hard to hold them back. Man, this is not okay. I cannot have this kid crying on me. I hate seeing people cry. It freaks me out. But I feel really sorry for him now. Fuck!

What the hell is happening to my life? I woke up this morning, happy, completely normal, completely ordinary and now look where I am. This is some seriously fucked up dream or something. It must be. Shit, now he's wiping his eyes with the end of his sleeve. I cannot deal with this. Ugh!

"Hey, listen, Jack, mate, look at me," I say, just spouting out whatever I can to get him to stop tearing up on me. "Don't ever, ever apologise for those idiots. Don't ever think for a second that you shouldn't be yourself. You hear me? You are a million times better than they will ever be."

"Yeah, right," he scoffs.

"I mean it, you are ten times the person they will ever be."

"You really mean that?"

"Of course I do, I wouldn't have said it if it wasn't true, would I?"

Well, I mean I don't really know the kid all that well to be honest, so, I probably would. Just to spare the awkwardness more so than anything else. But I'm not about to tell him that. I dont wan't him blubbering on me anymore. It is just too weird. I put my hand on his shoulder. Probably the wrong decision, considering, but fuck it, I'm just trying to be a good guy here. He looks at me with wet eyes, though looking a little happier than he did a few seconds previously.

"And, hey, I didn't get detention because of you. I got detention because I was stupid enough to grab that thing and run after you with it. It must have looked pretty funny though right? I mean me chasing after you with it."

He smiles at this. Humour. Good. Being funny always helps.

"And I'll let you in on a little secret, but you have to promise not to say anything okay?"

"Yeah, I promise."

"That was Dave's favourite toy. His nights are going to be pretty boring from now on."

His face breaks into a wide smile and he laughs a little at this. "You know you're the first person who has ever been truly nice to me," he says.

"Well, you know, kindness costs nothing," I say, quoting one of my granny's favourite mantras. "Better than spreading hate and bad vibes anyway."

He looks at my hand resting on his shoulder. I can

feel the heat coming from his body. Probably because of the heightened emotions running through him. I start to move it away but he stops me, placing his hand on top of mine. His hands are soft. His touch is gentle, nicer than I would have expected. He moves closer to me and I can see the freckles on the bridge of his nose that I didn't notice before. His eyes are blue and piercing, like they're staring straight into my soul. Also, I never noticed it until now, but up this close I can see how goodlooking he is. Suddenly I can't seem to understand why this kid is so unpopular. He is goodlooking. Incredibly clever. Sure he's a little weird, but isn't everyone? And to me right now he seems really cool.

His lips are moving but the sound doesn't penetrate my thoughts, so I don't know what he's saying. Don't care. I stare at him. Transfixed. He is leaning in closer now, his face not far from mine. His lips are red, plump, kind of inviting. He presses them against mine. Kissing me. I kiss him back. Just for a moment. I don't know why. There is just something, -it's, I dunno- it feels, well, natural, the smoothness of his lips feeling good against mine. I feel more comfortable, more relaxed now than I have all day. The tension built up in me is disa-

Wait, No! I can't. This is not right. I have a girlfriend.

I pull away. He looks at me, confused and I hesitate for a moment, not sure what to do. I pull my hand back, fast, clenching it tight and release it for the second time today, sending my fist crashing into another person's jaw. It sends him toppling to the ground, the dust and gravel underneath him flying in every direction.

"What the fuck are you playing at?" I bark at him.

"Nothing, I-I-I'm sorry. I didn't mean... I thought you wan-"

"Well you thought wrong. Stay away from me, you faggot!"

"Dean. Please. Wait!"

I don't wait. I can't. I turn and walk away, quickly, my heart racing, my hand throbbing. What the hell just happened? I speed away past the old distillery building, leaving Jack on the ground, cradling his arm. I think about turning back. Jimmy Browne and his gang might turn up and see Jack alone. Beat him up.

But I can't turn back.

Not now.

I keep going.

CHAPTER FIVE

The Letter

I head straight for my room when I get home, taking the stairs two at a time, nearly tripping a few times as my feet don't land properly on the narrow steps. I ignore the call of my name from the kitchen when whoever is home hears the door slamming shut behind me and the hurried footsteps going up the stairs.

Flicking the light switch on, I fling my bag into the corner beside my desk, where it crashes against the little metal bin. The empty water bottle that was perched on top of the pile of rubbish cascades to the floor. But I don't pick it up, instead kicking my shoes off, where they come to rest at the bottom of my bed. I sit on the edge of my matress, hunched forward, head in my hands, my mind running over everything that has happened so far today.

A buzzing in my pocket snaps me back into focus. My phone. I take it out, expecting to see Jack's name on the screen and I have to be honest I'm a little dissapointed when I see it isn't. It is just Karen. I slide the red decline button across, fully aware that it will probably come back to bite me on the ass later. But I don't feel like talking to anyone right now. And I don't know why I expected to see Jack's name or felt disappointed when I saw that it wasn't his name on the screen. Jack doesn't even have my number. What the hell is wrong with me? I am losing my fucking mind.

I get up and place my phone on my desk, noticing for the first time that my knuckles are starting to bruise up a little. I rub them with my other hand, pain pulsing through my fingers. My hands are not made for punching people in the jaw, I can tell you that much. That bruise is going to be there for days. It might stop me from being able to write. Damn.

But wait a minute! If I can get my mum to write me a letter for school, it might just get me out of having to do that punishment work for Miss Constance. Ha! Maybe it won't be so bad after all. What's a little pain for getting out of a one thousand word essay. I will take it. What is that saying again? You know the one. The cloud one. Every cloud has a silver lining? Yep that's it. I guess this is my measly silver lining for this horrible fuckfest of a day. God knows I need it.

I take my jumper, tie and shirt off and toss them onto the chair just in front of my desk, along with the dozens of other items of clothing that have come to rest there. I start to take to my trousers off but there is a knock at the door and my mum enters and closes the door behind her.

"Jesus, Mum, a little privacy please," I say, buttoning back up and starting to look for a clean t-shirt.

"Sit down, Dean."

The serious tone in her voice makes me look up and abandon the search for a clean t-shirt amongst the pile of clothes on the chair. She is holding a piece of paper in her hand. The Michael Hill Memorial emblem is just about visible at the top of the page. Fuck! I forgot Danvers said he was writing a letter home. It must have been hand delivered by the secretary though, because there is no way the post in this town would travel that fast. I can imagine the smug look on the old cow's face as she handed it to whoever opened the door, knowing that it would land me in a lot of trouble.

"Sit down Dean."

I do as my mum says, noticing the look of anger on her face and deciding that it will be better to cooperate. To try and make this as smooth as I can. I perch myself on the edge of my bed once again, crossing my arms in front of my bare chest, feeling somewhat vulnerable at the moment.

I wait for my mum to sit down beside me but she doesn't. I'm a bit taken aback when she doesn't. In the past, whenever she had come to scold me for my wrong doings, she would always sit beside me, maybe take my hand in hers and explain softly that I was in trouble. She would always end with a kiss on the forehead. This time is different though. I can already tell she won't be taking a soft approach today as she stays standing, looking at me intently. I bet Danvers made everything out to be a lot worse than it was in that letter of his. Wanker. And I suppose this is a much more embarrassing thing to have to give out to your son about.

"Well?" my mum says through gritted teeth, holding the letter out in front of her. "What is this all about Dean?"

"Er, it's a, er, letter. From Mr. Danvers I assume."

"Oh very astute of you, son. I can bloody well see that! But why am I receiving such a letter, Dean?"

"Because of, er, the thing that happened at school today."

"So, it's true then, is it? You brought that horrible *thing* into school and brandished it about in the corridors with another boy?"

"Well sort of, but, no not technically."

"What do you mean *not technically*? Did you or did you not wave it about in the corridors with a boy from your class?"

"Yeah, that bit is kind of true. But wait, Mum. Let me explain."

She closes her mouth and lets out a small sigh, folding her arms in front of her chest, the letter crumpling up between her fist and elbow. Without mentioning any names I launch into an abbreviated explanation, telling her about 'everything that happened'. I explain how 'a boy I don't know' was picking on 'another boy' from my class, waving that thing in his face and that I stepped into stop it from happening. I tell her that I grabbed that thing from his hand and that 'the other boy' from my class ran off and I chased after him to see if he was okay but a teacher caught us and thought we were after bringing it into school.

"But I didn't Mum, I swear. I wouldn't do anything like that. I was just trying to do the right thing, like you taught me to always do."

"You promise me it wasn't you who brought that thing into school?

"I promise Mum, it wasn't. It was some other guy. I don't know him. He must be in a different year to me or something."

"Okay, fine, I believe you." She smooths out the letter and reads it through. "It says here in the letter you have two weeks worth of detention?"

"Yep."

"And the other boy got the same?

"Er, yeah, I think he did."

I look down at the floor. I don't want my eyes to betray me. They can be quite telling sometimes, especially to my mum. I bet your mum can tell when you're lying too. It's like a weird superpower people suddenly develop when they become parents.

"And what about the boy who actually brought that thing into school? Did you tell Mr. Danvers who that was?"

"Er, no, I don't know his name."

"Well, first thing tomorrow morning you are to go straight to Mr. Danvers and tell him exactly what you told me. If you were just trying to do the right thing I'm sure he will understand. If not, well then you can just do the detention anyway. It will give you extra time to study and might help with your grades. We all know you could be getting better results, don't we?"

"Yes Mum."

I flash my winning smile at her, which she returns, though not as enthusiastically as I would like. I can tell, from what just transpired and what I told her about the events of today, that she knows I'm not being completely honest but that she does believe I *was* just trying to do the right thing.

"Dinner will be ready soon," she says, starting to pull pull open the door which she closed tight when she came in a few minutes ago.

"Mum"

I look down at my knuckles, remembering about asking her to write a letter to Miss Constance. But maybe I'd better not. I don't want to push my luck.

"Yes Dean?"

"Er- Can you not mention this whole thing to Dad? It's

a bit embarrassing."

"We'll see."

"Thanks Mum."

When the door clicks shut I take my trousers off. I don't even bother looking for clean clothes to change into. I just pick up my phone from the desk and flop myself down onto my bed in just my boxers. Entering the pin code to unlock it, I see there are three missed calls and a voicemail message from Karen. Dialling the voicemail service, I raise the phone to my ear and listen to the message. Nothing important. Just wondering where I am, why I'm not answering my phone, it's not like me, yada, yada, yada. I don't feel like talking to her right now so I just type out a quick text message:

Got detention, plus 1000 word essay from Corporal Constance. Only home now. Gonna be up all night doing it. Talk tomorrow x

I hit send and hope that she just accepts it for what it is. But that would be just too much to ask for today, wouldn't it! No more than thirty seconds later a text comes through from Karen:

Only home now? Where did u go? x

I cannot catch a fucking break today. I write back quickly:

Met Jack H on the way. Talked to him for a bit x

I leave out the part about Jack crying. I leave out the part about me punching Jack. But most importantly I leave out the part about the, um, kiss thing. Obviously.

Jack H? As in Jack Hawkins?

The very same. Just said sorry for what Dave did to him x

Oh. Yeah Dave told me what he did and said that u punched him. That wasnt cool

Oh he did, did he? But, hold on... when was she talking

to Dave? They don't share any classes? And they are only ever together when I'm around. And have you noticed she stopped sending little x's? I have.

I know thats why I punched him

I meant u punching Dave. Hes ur best friend

Is she serious? I sit up straight on my bed, crossing my legs and tucking my feet under my thighs, my thumbs working frantically. Is she really sticking up for Dave in this situation?

Are u for real Karen? Dave was bullying some innocent kid and ur sticking up for him? Have u lost ur mind?

Dont talk to me like that Dean. Im not sticking up for him. Im just saying u shouldnt have punched Dave. U both did something wrong

I did something wrong? This has got to be some sort of joke right? This is Karen, *my* girlfriend. She is supposed to be on *my* side. Not Dave's. I need to think carefully about what to write back. I don't want to start a full blown argument with her but she has to realise I did the right thing in this situation. I start typing but a shout from downstairs saying dinner is ready snaps me back to my senses. Deleting what I have typed, I write instead:

Just about to have dinner. Dont wanna fight. Talk tomorrow

Okay see u tomorrow

Love u

No reply.

I know that should probably have some adverse effect on me.

It doesn't.

CHAPTER SIX

Attraction

Dinner is as normal and boring as it usually is. Frozen fish, mashed potatoes and mushy peas scooped out of a tin and heated almost to death in the microwave. Darren, my older brother by seven years, comes in as we are half way through. He takes his dinner out of the oven where Mum left it to keep warm and joins us at the table. The chat is pretty standard stuff. Dad tells us about his day. Darren tells us about the new footballs they got in at the sports shop he works in at the local shopping centre. FIFA approved or some shit like that.

Mum hasn't said anything to my dad about what happened at school today or about the letter she received from Mr. Danvers. Thank Goodness for small mercies, right? (No, I don't know either. It's just something my Granny used to say. Seems quite apt though). Don't think I could handle my dad knowing about everything that happened. It is bad enough that my mum knows. And I'm pretty sure the whole school will know by now or at least they will by tomorrow. Especially now that Karen knows. She will spread it around, I'm sure. She always was a bit of a gossip. But I'll just have to deal with that when and if it comes to it. And I'm also pretty sure Darren knows, judging by the smirk he gives me as I load my plate into the dishwasher and head into the living room.

I watch some TV for a while but I can't really concentrate on anything so I decide to head up to the bathroom, to have a shower. I take my time washing myself, mulling over, once again, everything that happened today. The warm water shooting from the shower head cascades down my back. It's quite soothing after the day I've had. Seriously, how can my life get so fucked up in just one day? Not even twenty four hours and my whole world has gone completely topsy turvy. Not even twenty four hours ago I had a perfectly happy, perfectly normal life. I had freinds who I never would have even thought about punching. But then again they wouldn't normally be such assholes. I had a girlfriend that would have been on my side no matter what.

Now I'm not sure where I stand with her anymore. But the one thing that my mind keps returning to, the one thing that I keep trying hard not to think about is the fact that Jack kissed me. But that's not why I keep thinking about it. Not really. I keep thinking about it because I think I liked it. I know that sounds totally fucked up and everything but when it happened, I have to be honest, it felt good. It felt natural. I know it shouldn't have, I have a girlfriend who I love, (I mean, I think I love, I'm not really sure anymore) but it did. And that is totally fucking with my head.

I step out of the shower, grab the nearest towel and start to dry myself off, stopping when I catch a glimpse of myself in the mirror. I stand in front of it and examine myself closely, leaning in closer over the sink and looking at my face intently. There is something different about me, though I can't really put my finger on it. I look exactly the same as I did when I woke up this morning, my damp hair hanging down over my forehead as it usually does, my shoulders sloping down at their usual awkward angle, my arms hanging limply by my sides. But when I really look at myself, I mean really stare into my soul, I can notice it, I can feel it, bubbling away deep in my gut.

I look down as I wrap the towel around my waist. The bruising on my knuckles has really come through now. I lift my hand up in front of my face, the purply, blue-ish colour contrasting against my otherwise pale skin. Looking past my hand to my face in the mirror again, I notice how my lips also contrast against my pale skin. Red, plump. Like Jack's. I bring my hand up and touch them with the tips of my index and middle fingers. I close my eyes and think about how good Jack's lips felt pressed against mine. How I could taste his swe-

No! Stop! I shake my head, forcing any thoughts of Jack out of my mind. I can't keep doing this. Turning away from the mirror, I wrench the door open and head down the hallway to my room so I can finish drying myself and get some clean clothes on. A call from my brother's room stops me in my tracks.

"Hey, Beanie, come here."

Yeah "Beanie", that's me. Well only to my knob of a brother. It's just a nickname he has been calling me since we were younger. Something to do with the fact he couldn't pronounce Dean properly when he was a kid. So it just kind of stuck. Luckily only with him though. No one else calls me it. And that is definitely not a bad thing, I can tell you. Fucking "Beanie".

I poke my head around his bedroom door and see him sitting on his bed, his tablet on his lap, music playing quietly from the docking station on his bedside table.

"Whats up? I wanna get dressed."

"What's up he says. What's up? Why dont you tell me "W*hat's up*" Beanie?"

"Guess Mum told you what happened then," I say laughing and taking a seat on the end of his bed, the towel wrapped around me bunching up around my waist.

"That she did." He raises his eyebrows at me. "Is it true?"

"Depends what she told you. Have you told Dad?"

"Have I told Dad? Tut, tut Beanie, what do you take me for? Of course I haven't told Dad. I presume you would actually like to keep being able to leave the house, wouldn't you."

"Thanks. Daz!"

"Oi, don't be calling me that!"

I know he hates being called Daz. It's what his ex- girlfriend used to call him. And that was a nasty break up. So anything that even slightly reminds him of her winds him up terrible. It's great.

"Oh, why not Daz? Don't you like being called Daz, *Daz*?"

"Shut it you!"

He takes a pillow out from behind his back and sends it flying straight for my head. I duck out of the way just in time and it falls to the floor at the end of the bed with a soft thud.

"Alright I won't call you Daz anymore" I say, laughing. "Lest the floor should receive any more beatings from your pillows."

"Speaking of beatings," he says, eyeing me over the top of his knees. "What happened to your hand? Wasn't Jimmy Browne and his gang was it? Saw them hanging around by the distillery on my way home earlier."

Wait, at the distillery? That is where I left Jack, alone, after I punched him. I hope he got away from there before they showed up. If he didn't he would have been in real trouble. Shit!

"Oh, really, what were they doing?" I try to sound as nonchalant as I can. "They weren't beating anyone up were they?"

"No, they were just smoking and shit."

Thank fuck for that, I wouldn't be able to live with myself if I found out he ran afoul of Jimmy and his gang because of me. Darren narrows his eyes at me. He knows I'm hiding something.

"Do I need to pay him a visit?" he asks me.

"What?"

"Jimmy and his gang. Is that what happened to your hand?"

"Oh, no, that was Dave."

"Dave? As in your best mate, 'can't separate the two of you' Dave?"

"Yeah, I punched him." I don't mention anything about also punching Jack.

"Why?"

"He was the one that brought the dildo into school and start bullying another kid with it."

"So you punched him?"

"Yeah, he was being a dick."

"Being a dick was he?" Darren laughs. It takes me a few seconds to realise the joke.

"Haha, very funny, moron. I'm going to bed."

"Coolio, Beanie, just try not get into any more trouble yeah?"

I stand up and head for the door, readjusting the towel

around my waist. I really need to put some fucking clothes on.

"No problemo *Daz*," I say with a wink and dash out of the room before the floor falls victim to another pillow attack.

I get back to my room and fish out a clean t-shirt and pair of shorts, before taking my laptop out and powering it up. I have a one thousand word essay on "The Merits of Sleep" remember. Due at the start of detention time tomorrow. How the hell am I supposed to write one thousand words on that? I sit down on my bed, my laptop resting on my thighs and open up a word document. I type out my first sentence. I just begin to type out the second sentence when there's a PING and a little bubble pops up in the bottom right corner of the screen.

1 New Message from Dave Rudden.

I press the little red x above it, clearing it off the screen.

I don't want to talk to Dave right now. What he did to Jack today was not like him at all. He was a real asshole.

I go back to typing but another PING comes through and the little bubble pops back up.

Dave. Again.

I click on the little x. Again.

I try to go back to typing my essay but I can't concentrate. I'm expecting another PING to come through any second. If there is one thing to be said for Dave Rudden it is that he never gives up. I stare at the screen for a few minutes but it remains message free. Good. Looks like he got the hint. I will see him at school tomorrow anyway.

But fuck, I can't concentrate on this essay. The Merits of Sleep. What kind of a fucking essay topic is that? Maybe after I've had some myself I'll be able to do it better. However, more out of habit than actually meaning to, I find my hand whizzing over the mousepad and clicking open my Facebook page. I usually do every night anyway, checking it just before I go to sleep.

This time, however, instead of just scrolling through the newsfeed, I find myself hovering the cursor over the search bar. I type in a *J*. A list of names show up; Jenna, Jake, John, Josh. I follow up the *J* with an *a*. Nope, still just Jake, Jacob etc. I go with *c* next and when I don't see what I'm looking for I finally type in a *k*. I look down through the list of Jack's that have shown up. Johnson, Willis, Daniels. Todea. Nope. Not there.

Finally, at about two results from the bottom and several minutes of scrolling, I see it. *Jack Hawkins*. I click the little thumbnail and it takes me to a profile. I lean in forward look at the profile picture. It's definitely him. I scroll down a little bit. A little notice tells me we have zero mutual friends. Not surprising. But it is surprising that his profile is on public. I thought it would have surely been on private. I suppose he probably doesn't get many people searching for his name so he doesn't feel the need to put any protections on it. I see that his last post was two days ago. I scroll further. I come to a group of photos uploaded by Jack a few months ago. By the looks of them they are from a recent holiday with his family. I click into them. No harm in just taking a quick look. I click through a few of them and come to a stop when I get to a shirtless picture of Jack on the beach and my jaw hits the floor at record speed.

What the actual, actual fuck! This kid is super fucking fit. Look at that fucking six pack! How the hell have I never noticed that before? Well I suppose I've never seen him out of his uniform before. But damn, you would think I would have been able to tell just by looking at him. Whenever I've seen him at school the kid always looks all shy and introverted, like he couldn't even beat up a teddy bear. But shit, the kid is rippped.

I press the little arrow to go to the next picture. Another shirtless one from his holidays. Closer this time. I can see the sweat (or water possibly) glistening on his chest in this one. Glistening on his smooth, bronze coloured, sun kissed skin. I look up at his face. He's smiling, a perfect smile. Those, plump, red lips. Imagine what they would feel li-

I slam my laptop shut and push it away from me. What the fuck is wrong with me? What the hell am I saying? I get up, leave my laptop on my desk, walk backwards and forwards frantically beside my bed for a few seconds, eventually coming to a stop and turning off the light. I slip my t-shirt off and climb into bed, pulling the duvet up around my chin.

I turn over onto my left side, close my eyes and try to empty my mind of everything but as I begin to drift off to sleep a horrible realisation snaps me back into consciousness, the force of it hitting me as hard as the punches I threw today hit their intended targets...

...I think I fucking fancy Jack Hawkins.

CHAPTER SEVEN

Noticeable Absence

I wake up with a start, to the sound of my mum calling my name from the bottom of the stairs, feeling sticky, sweat pooled under my armpits and clinging to my chest. I rub my eyes and look at the alarm clock on my bedside table. The little red numbers show that it's 7:45am.

"I'm awake," I shout back groggily to my mum who has called out (well, practically shouted) my name again.

I flop my head back down onto my pillow and try to recall the dream I was prematurely yanked out of. Do you ever get that? When you wake up you can instantly re-member your dream but even after just a few seconds it starts to fade and disappear from your memory? That is what's happening to me now. I try hard to remember the details, my brain scrambling to latch on to the smallest recollection. But I'm struggling to grasp anything, it is slipping away too quickly.

It must not have been worth remembering, so I fling the duvet off my body, slide out of bed and see my laptop on the table where I left it the night before. I hesitate for a moment, thinking about whether to open it up, look again at the Facebook page that I remember was left open when I slammed it shut last night. But I don't. Instead, I turn away and make my way downstairs. The cereal and milk are already laid out on the table in the kitchen when I walk in, my mum standing over by the sink, a mug of tea in her hand.

"Morning sweetheart."

"Morning," I grunt back.

I grab the box of cereal and empty some of its contents into a bowl. I pour some milk in on top of that and start shovelling large spoonfuls into my mouth.

This is a new day. Forget about yesterday. What happened was just a tiny blip. Time to start over. I look down at my hand holding the spoon, at my knuckles, a yellow tinge now starting to mix in with the purple bruising. Can I just start over as easily as that? Can I just go back to school and act like none of it even happened? For starters will Dave even still want to be my friend? I mean I did punch the guy pretty hard and then I just flat out ignored his messages.

And Karen. I have no idea what is going to happen there. I expect everything will be fine though. When she hears what I have to say and realises *I* was doing the right thing she will be on my side. I hope.

And fucking Jack Hawkins. I just have to steer clear of him, sit as far away from him as possible in every class, not even spare him a look and just hope he doesn't say anything about what happened at the distillery. But who is he going to tell anyway? The kid is a loner, even with his hot, sculpted body and perfect smi-

"I'm not going to ask you again, Dean."

"Huh?"

I realise someone is talking to me and look up to see my mum standing about a foot away from me, my PE trainers dangling from the laces she has draped across the tips of her fingers.

"What is wrong with you, Dean? You look completely zoned out."

"Oh, er, nothing I'm fine. Yeah I need them," I say, acknowledging the trainers. "I have PE today. Just leave them by the door. I'll grab them on my way out."

"Okay, but you need to get your act together Dean. Start paying attention and for the love of God don't get into anymore trouble at school."

"I won't Mum, I promise. I'm just tired."

"Good," she says, her eyes searching my face for signs of... well, I don't know what really... but it would be nothing good, I can tell you.

Not wanting to give her any more chances to read something from my expression, I finish the last dregs of cereal from the bowl and pop it into the dishwasher along with the spoon and head back upstairs to get changed into my school uniform. I throw on the shirt from yesterday. It is still good for another wear. Then I put on my trousers, shoes, tie and jumper. I know, it is a huge pain in the ass having to wear a uniform every single day. But I haven't got a choice. Them's the rules of Michael Hill Memorial. Every item of uniform has to be worn every day and must be worn properly or face the consequences.

I comb my hair into a relatively neat style, grab my laptop form the desk and open it up. I type in my password and up pops Jack's facebook page. Shit. I forgot for a second that that would be the first thing popping up. I minimise that window rather than closing it down completely and open up the messages that Dave sent last night. I don't even bother reading them properly, just scanning through them, the words 'sorry' and 'asshole' jumping out at me. Several times actually.

I type a short message offering my apologies and say that I will see him today at lunch, hit send then shut the laptop down and leave it on the desk. I grab my schoolbag from the floor beside the bin, pack my PE gear into it, run down the stairs, grab my trainers that my mum left near the door, shout a goodbye to her in the kitchen, yank open the door and step out into the cold autumn air.

I get to shool a little before 9:00am. The corridors are packed full of students waiting for the bell to ring and the teachers to come, so that they can race in and take their seats in the classrooms. Not because they are lazy or any-thing and canot bear the prospect of having to stand for more than 10 minutes. No, no they are all just so eager to learn. Yeah and I'm in the running to be the next Pope!

I squeeze my way through the throng of teenagers, heading to room B12 where I have Geography first thing with Miss Dolan. For a school that doesn't have a huge student population, they always seem to take up the en-tire corridors, spreading like a nasty heat rash on a warm day. I just about manage to make my way by a particu-larly loud group of giggling first year girls when I spot Dave and Karen at the end of the corridor. I start to make my way towards them but...wait... are they...

I backtrack a little and duck behind a short, rather ro-tund boy who is looking at me like I have just stolen some food from right out of his mouth. He starts to move away from me but I grab him by the elbow.

"Stay where you are," I whisper.

"What? Geroff me ya weirdo," he says, trying to yank his elbow out of my grip.

"See those two holding hands down there." I incline my head in the direction of Karen and Dave.

"Yeah wharra 'bout them?"

"That's my girlfriend and my best friend."

"Oh-h-h-h man, that is rough."

"So you can see it too then?"

"Yeah, man. Looks like she's been doin' the dirty on ya man."

Fucking hell. Now I know why she was sticking up for Dave last night. She has been fucking him behind my back. My best friend. The guy wo encouraged me and Karen to get together in the first place. I have known him for thirteen fucking years. And he goes and does this? I really regret not punching the fucker a lot harder now. I should have made sure he was out for the count.

But it is all starting to make sense now. It's becoming clear, to me at least. I bet he only encouraged me to get with Karen so that he could be close to her every day. And I bet the reason he has been acting like such an ass-hole lately is because he's been seeing Karen and he's been struggling to hide his guilt. And that struggle has been manifesting itself in his dickery. And when I asked him yesterday what his problem was he could barely look at me. Now I know why.

I wonder how lon-

"Hey, man."

I feel a tugging at my hand. I look up and see that I am still gripping the fat boy tightly at the elbow. The corridor is starting to empty as people make their way into the classrooms on either side. I look down to the end of the corridor but there'snothing to see, just a blank wall where Dave and Karen were standing a minute ago.

"Man, the bell went. I need to get to class."

"Oh yeah, sorry," I say, releasing his elbow. I hadn't even heard the bell going. "Er, thanks for, er, letting me hide behind you."

"No problem man, good luck with that whole situation."

He waddles off through the nearest door and I am left standing in the corridor by myself. I make my way quickly to room B12 where I slip in behind the rest of my classmates and take my seat at the left hand side of the classroom. I take out my notebook and pen, placing them side by side on the table in front of me. Miss Dolan calls the register from her desk and when she is finished proceeds to power up the overhead projector, where an image of an oxbow lake flashes onto the screen at the top of the room.

"Following on from our last lesson, can anyone recap for me, briefly, how oxbow lakes are formed?" She directs her question to no one in particular, giving anyone that knows the opportunity to proffer up an answer.

And come on, that's simple. An oxbow lake is formed when a meander is created in a river due to the erosion of the bank and after a long period of time the meander becomes very curved and eventually narrows and cuts through during a flood, cutting off the meander and forming the oxbow.

But I'm not going to raise my hand to answer. No way. I will leave that to someone else. I lower my head and look at the years of scribbles etched onto at the surface of my desk, waiting for someone to offer up an answer. I bet it will be Jack. He is always the first one with his hand in the air any time a question is asked. But there is a few moments of deathly silence that follows Miss Dolan's question which makes me raise my head. I look up to the desk right at the top of the room, where Jack usually sits. He's not there. The chair is empty.I look around the room. Just to see if he has decided to change seats for some reason. But nope, he hasn't moved seats. He's not in the room.

That is really weird. Jack Hawkins, to my knowledge, has never, ever missed a day of school. Why would he start now? Not because of me surely? It can't be. He wouldn't miss school because of that, would he? No, it must be something serious. Maybe I punched him too hard and he has a broken jaw or something. But nah, he can't have. I am definitely not that strong. Maybe it's something more serious...

Didn't Darren say he saw Jimmy Browne and his gang hanging around the distillery last night after I got home? What if they got there just as Jack was leaving? They would have beat him up really badly. Fuck! It's the only explanation. He is probably lying in a hospital bed right now, fighting for his life. And it's all my fucking fault. Crap! What have I done?

Sweat is beginning to build up on the palms of my hands so I rub them on the legs of my trousers, my chest starting to feel really tight. I can't breathe. I think I'm having a panic attack. I have to get out of here. Like right now. I raise my hand into the air, fast, with force, making the person sitting to the right of me jump a little in their seat.

"Yes Dean?

"Miss, can I go to the bathroom please, I feel really ill."

She must see that I'm not faking it because her eyes widen and she nods her head, probably praying to God that I dont puke all over her classroom.

"Yes, yes of course, go. Quickly!"

"Thanks Miss."

I grab my stuff off the table and stuffing it into my

bag that I took up from the floor at my feet, I practically sprint out of the room. The noise of the door snapping shut behind me only reaches my ears as I turn at the end of the corridor. My heavy footsteps ring out through the empty corridor as I zip through it, down the stairs and charge headfirst into the nearest bathroom. Breathing hard, my chest heaving, I dash over to the sink closest to me and turn on the taps, splashing the cold water up into my face.

Calm down, I think to myself. Just fucking calm down. You are over-reacting. Big time. Jack is fine. He has to be. He is probably just running late. Yeah that's it. Definitely. He is just running a little late. There is nothing to be worried about. He will waltz in a bit later and everything will be fine...Won't it?

I stand hunched over the sink, my hands gripping either side of it and wait for my breathing to return to normal. I turn the taps off then, halting the flow of water and plunging the bathroom into total silence. I stroll into the nearest cubicle and grab a few sheets of toilet paper and begin to dry the excess water off my face and hands. As I'm doing so, I hear the door to the bathroom squeak open and a voice I recognise instantly says behind me:

"Oi Turner, not up to any funny business I hope."

CHAPTER EIGHT

Divergence

I spin around on my heels to face Dave Rudden. My best friend. My best friend who has been sleeping with my girlfriend for fuck knows how long. I look at him standing there, bold as brass, a big smile on his stupid little face, slight bruising around his jaw where I punched him yesterday. Completely oblivious to the fact that I know his dirty little secret.

Ha! I say that like I don't have some of my own. But my dirty little secrets are not important right now. They are something that can be dealt with later. What is important now though, is that I get the truth. Before I make up my mind. Well, I think I already had my mind made up when I saw them together this morning, and after these feelings I have been having about Jack, coupled with the fact that we haven't been as happy as we were in the beginning, I am sure now that it has to be done. But this will definitely confirm whether it's the right decision or not.

Dave raises his hand and clicks his fingers in front of my face a few times. "Are you in there Turner?"

"What?"

"You look completely zoned out of it. Are you on

something?"

"What? No. Don't be stupid. I'm grand."

"Well, you look like you're on something," Dave says to me as he walks over to the nearest urinal. "If you are you better share it."

I hear the zip of his trousers being pulled down and a second later the unmistakable sound of the spray of urine echoes out through the room, as it hits the once white but now practically mustard coloured porcelain. I lift my bag up from the ground near the sink where I dropped it when I came in and sling it over my shoulder, gripping the strap so it doesn't slide off. I stare at Dave's back as he continues to piss, the stream still flowing strong. I have to do it now. I have to ask. I'm not sure yet how I am going to react, but I don't care. I have to know, for real, that I am making the right decision. So that I can begin to deal with these fucked up feelings I've been having.

"How long has it been going on?"

I direct the question at the back of his head, waiting for him to turn around. After a quick shake he zips up and turns around to face me, a slight look of confusion on his face.

"What you talking bout Turner? How long has what been going on?"

"Don't treat me like an idiot Dave. We've been friends for far too long. Don't lie to me. I know." I stuff the hand that's not holding my bag into my pocket and half angle my head towards the ground but keeping my eyes on Dave.

He looks at me and starts to laugh a little. "You know what?"

"Just answer the question Dave," I say, curling my

pocketed hand into a fist. I don't want to get angry, because looking now at Dave and thinking about Karen and how distant she has seemed lately, I'm realising that I'm not all that bothered by it, to be completely honest, but the fact he is still trying to hide it, when I'm clearly calling him out on it, is starting to piss me off.

"Are you sure you're not fucking on something Turner? I haven't a clue what you're talking about. Stop talking in riddles."

Fine. If he is going to play the idiot then it just needs to be said bluntly. "I saw you. This morning. Holding hands. And kissing."

"You saw...."

"Yeah I saw. Upstairs. In the corridor. You could have at least tried to hide it. You must've known someone would see. You obviously didn't expect it to be me though."

The smile that was on his face a moment ago falls off, quickly. It's replaced by a look of shock and something else. I'm not sure what it is, but he looks... almost ashamed. The heat that was beginning to rise up my neck dissipates and my fist unfurls. I hold it flat against my thigh and take a step closer to him. He must think I am going to swing for him or something because he starts to back away. So I take my hand out of my pocket and raise it in front of me, fingers spread open, palm facing forward.

"Ha, relax will you, I'm not going to hit you, stud."

"You're... you're not?"

"Nope, I promise." I lower my arm and let it hang by my side.

His face flickers through a mixture of expressions, but confusion seems to be the most dominant one at the moment. It is pretty funny actually. Dave Rudden could beat me senseless in a heartbeat but now, here he is, cowering away. From me. Dean Turner. Mr. Average himself. I must have hit him pretty hard yesterday to warrant this sort of reaction from him. I lean my ass up against the sink and gesture for Dave to do the same at the one next to me. We sit in silence for a few minutes.

Finally I ask again. "So how long has it been going on? And I want the truth Dave. Please."

"Well... er, she started texting me about, a- a month ago, saying how you weren't giving her any attention, how you always seemed to be interested in everything and anything except her. Then we, er, started meeting up before school, before she would go and see you." I can hear what I believe is genuine remorse in his voice, the words just barely escaping from his mouth. He takes a gulp and looks me in the eye. "I'm really, really sorry Turner. I shouldn't have done it. I don't know what I was thinking. She just seemed like she needed someone to talk to and before I knew it-"

I gesture with my hand for him to stop and he trails off into silence. I don't want to hear the details. I don't need to. I've heard enough. I knew deep down that she wasn't happy. And now my mind is made up. When I see her at lunch today I will talk to her. End it. I stand up straight and turn to face Dave.

"Is she happy? When she's with you?"

"Er, yeah, I think so."

"Good, she's great, really. Just, like, be better than I was."

I have said all I can. Well, all I'm willing to say. I turn, starting to walk away, but Dave calls me back.

"Wait. I don't understand. Aren't you angry? Don't you want to hit me?"

"Well, no, not really. What would be the point?" I ask.

"I dont know. But you must care at least?"

"Of course I care, I'd be a right dick if I didn't care, but I've got other stuff going on that I need to deal with. And I kinda knew she wasn't happy for a couple of weeks now actually. She's been a bit distant with me. But I didn't think she'd been seeing someone else. And especially not you. I'm surprised that you would do something like that to me. I mean, you're my best friend."

"I know, I'm really, really sorry. I mean it. I've been wanting to come clean for ages. Since the beginning really, before anything even really happened. But one thing led to another and it became this big thing and then I was afraid of how you would react. And now I'm even more afraid because you're so calm."

"It doesn't matter now anyway. Like I said, I have something else that I need to deal with right now."

"So we're good then?"

"Well I'm not going to flip out but I wouldn't say we're good at the moment either. You've done a really shitty thing and I'm not sure I forgive you yet. So I think we probably shouldn't be around each other for a few days or something. But we'll be fine in a bit. Just do one thing for me. Don't say anything until I see her at lunch. You owe me that much at least."

"No, I mean yeah, of course, Turner."

"Good. Catch you later."

Now I turn and walk out the door, leaving Dave standing by the sink, probably more confused than ever. Everything I said was true. I am not angry as such. Just disappointed really. I'm sure I will forgive him, in time. I don't really care that he has been sleeping with Karen. It's more the betrayal by my closest friend that irks me more. But I have other shit to deal with. I have to find out why Jack isn't at school today. Plus I'm going to have to see Karen at lunch and break up with her. I'm not relishing the thought of it to be honest. I suspect it will be pretty bad. I just hope she doesn't cry. You know I hate people crying on me.

I look down at my watch. Only ten minutes left of Geography with Miss Dolan so there is no point heading back to that really. She probably won't be expecting me back anyway. Probably thinks I've gone home ill. Instead I head to the next class, where I hang around outside for the remaining ten minutes, examining some of the posters that adorn the walls of the corridor. Some about anti-bullying, some about mental and physical well-being, others about the best ways to study. None of them are very accurate or insightful but all are very large, very bold, very brightly coloured. Definitely eye catching. When the bell rings and the students in the class are finished pouring out, I go inside and take my seat. On the left hand side of the room, of course.

I keep my head down for most of the class, only looking up to see if Jack has slipped into his seat in front of the teacher's desk. He hasn't. A fresh wave of panic begins to descend over me. It doesnt look like he's coming in today does it? But I can't think about that right now.

Pushing that aside and controlling my breathing, I think about what I'm going to say to Karen. How best to put it. How easy I should make it. It isn't her fault really. She wasn't happy being with me so she had to seek solace in the arms of another. It is just a shame that it had to be my best friend. But my life seems so fucked up right now, that it really doesn't surprise me.

The bell rings, signalling the end of the double class,

so I gather up my stuff and head down to the cafeteria, where most of the seats have already been occupied by ravenous teenagers. I spot Karen chatting animatedly to some other girls around a table in the far right corner. Time to do it I suppose.

CHAPTER NINE

No Updates

So I did it. But I won't bore you with all the details of the break up. To be honest it was far more amicable than I would have expected. When I went over and tapped her on the shoulder and told her we needed to talk she didn't look at all surprised. Dave had probably already texted her, even though I had asked him not to say anything. It doesn't matter though. At least now she will be happy (I hope) and bonus, there were no tears. It is always good when there are no tears. Anyway, we went our separate ways (although I'm sure we'll keep in touch. You can't just erase seven months out of existence like that) and I had lunch by myself.

It was a weird experience. I have never had to have lunch by myself before. Ever. There is usually someone around. I didn't even see Luke, my other close friend. I am willing to bet my entire life's savings that Dave and Karen have been talking to him. Telling him to steer clear in case I explode. Probably thinking to themselves that I'm far too calm after what just happened. But don't worry, I'm not going to explode. I am fine. Honestly. I actually feel a little better. Like a weight I didn't even know was pressing down on top of me has been lifted. I feel better equipped to deal with the fucked up thoughts I went to sleep with yesterday. Not that I am about to go shouting it from the rooftops. You must be joking. I don't even really know what the deal is there yet. It's going to take some time to figure all that shit out.

After lunch I had PE. It passed without incident. Thank fuck for that. Though I didn't participate as enthusiastically as I usually do. I have way too much on my mind. Namely Jack and all that mixed up shit. I need to know that he is okay, why he didn't turn up for schol today. And it's not like I can just go up to Jimmy Browne (who I tackled a little more aggressively than usual during football, you know, just in case) and ask if he put him in hospital. It would be way too suspicious. But if something has happened and he is hurt because of me I'll never be able to live with myself.

It is the last class of the day now. History with Mr. Usher. Usher is hands down the most boring teacher I have ever had the misfortune of encountering. He doesn't even try to make the subject interesting. He just settles for reciting dates and facts, often without even putting them into context.

A knock on the door makes everyone, including myself, look up. A first year girl enters and hands a note to him. She saunters back out slowly, looking around at the group of seventeen year olds that are staring at her with a scowl and closes the door quietly behind her, while Usher reads the note silently.

"Okay then. Anyone that will be serving detention today is to report to the usual room, that being B17. And if for some reason you cannot remeber whether you are one of said perpetrators or not, Miss Constance will be waiting at the main doors to provide you with a gentle reminder. Now back to the Third Reich. Can anyone tell me, when did...."

Oh Fucking Hell! I forgot about the fact that I have detention. Stupid. But come on, you can't really blame me can you? I had so much going on today that it completely went out of my mind.

And fuck, to top it all off, I have just remembered I have an essay due for Miss Constance at the start of today's detention! I look up at the clock above Mr. Usher's head at the top of the room. There is no way I am going to be able to get it done now. Detention starts in twenty minutes.

I lower my head back down and look at the pen clutched in my hand. My knuckles are still quite bad looking. I might be able to say that it impeded my ability to write. But... this is Miss Constance we are talking about here. She is not likely to buy a bullshit excuse like that. I guess I will just have to take whatever extra punishment she throws at me. It is my own fault anyway. I should have finished it last night. But nooo, I had to go and get distracted didn't I? Ugh, I wish my life would hurry up and get back to normal. I'm not sure I can handle any more bizzare changes.

When the bell rings out through the school at the end of class, signalling the end of the day, I make my way to room B17, where half a dozen other kids are standing outside. Each one solemn faced, looking about as happy to be there as I am. I get chatting to a kid I recognise from being here yesterday. He tells me that he 'got sent down' (his words not mine) for no reason. That the teachers have a target on his head. Not bloody likely I can't help thinking to myself! One look at him and you can tell he is a trouble maker. Although I don't say this to him, obviously. I just nod along in agreement.

"So what did you get sent down for?" he asks me.

I open my mouth to reply but don't get a chance to as Corporal Constance comes around the corner and lets everyone into the room. I start to walk by her but she puts her hand out and stops me from entering. She ushers me to the side with a flick of her wrist, to let the remaining few students into the room.

"Good afternoon, Mr. Turner," she says, holding out her hand. "I take it your essay is completed and is up to an acceptable standard?"

"Er, no, Miss, sorry."

"Excuse me?" Her eyes are nearly bulging out of her head, her lips pursed tightly together, as if she's just been forced to swallow a glass of pure, raw lemon juice.

"I, er, haven't got it done Miss. Sorry."

"Oh dear me. What is the excuse? Death in the family? House burned down? Are you going to tell me that it has something to do with that bruise on your hand?"

What a bitch! Eyes like a hawk. But there goes any hope of pulling an excuse out of my back pocket. I will just have to be honest. Well... semi-honest.

"No Miss, I, er, just forgot to do it."

"You. Just. Forgot. To. Do. It."

"Yes Miss."

"Well, that is just not acceptable, is it Mr. Turner?"

"No Miss."

She looks down at her hands where the book containing the names of all the students who have received detention resides, a little *too* comfortably I might add. She flicks through a number of pages. As she does so a sly smirk crosses her face before falling away swiftly to be replaced by a look of pure contentment.

"Oh, would you look at that! I see you are already set to serve two weeks worth of detention. How about we add another week onto that?" She scribbles something down, the pen moving frantically across the page. "Yes, that seems fitting. And I expect that essay to be completed by tomorrow. You may even begin now. If your poor, injured hand will allow it. Now in you go. Quickly!"

She gestures stiffly towards the open door of the classroom. I hurry in past her and take a seat just behind the guy I was chatting to outside who turns in his seat and rolls his eyes as if to say 'what a bitch'. I concur!

Corporal Constance sits herself down at the teachers desk and begins to call out the names of the students that are supposed to be here today. When she gets to my name I give a feeble reply of "Here" and proceed to take out my pen and notebook and start to write, trying to remember what I had begun typing last night. The Merits of Sleep are....

"Jack?"

Silence.

"Jack Hawkins?"

My head shoots up at the sound of the name.

"Does anyone know where Jack Hawkins is?"

No answer.

"Hmpf" She makes a note in the stupid little book.

But shit, I forgot Jack was supposed to be in detention today too. Now I know something must be seriously wrong, because there is no way a perfect student like Jack would miss detention and not even let the school know about it. Not that he should even be getting detention in the first place.

My chest feels a little tight. I put the pen I'm holding down on the table and place my hands on my knees, taking a few deep breaths until it returns to normal. I can't let panic affect me now. I have to concentrate.

I hear the scraping of chair legs on the floor and Constance begins her usual patrolling of the aisles, looking in on people's work. I grab my pen up off the table and begin to scribble down what I can remember starting last night. I sense her walk past my shoulder, where she lingers for a few moments, though she remains silent, before passing on to the next desk.

I write for the duration of the detention session, not sure if I am getting anywhere near to the one thousand word target or if it even makes any sense. Although it doesn't really matter does it? It is just a punishment exercise. It's not like it is going to be selected for publication in any scientific journals. Finally, as my hand starts to cramp up, Corporal Constance announces that time is up and we may go home. Good. It feels like my hand is about to fall off. Just as I'm stuffing my things into my bag, Corporal Constance approaches my desk where she stops and taps her foot. Tap, tap, tap. Bloody hell, what does she want now? Can't she just leave me alone?

"I see you have been writing for the entire duration," she says to me. "I'm sure you have written enough by now and the message has been well received. I am willing to accept it now."

Well that's surprising. I was not expecting that at all. She must be going soft in her old age, the frumpy old cow.

"Oh, er, yeah okay," I say, tearing the sheets of paper from my notebook and handing them to her. "And the extra week's detention?"

"Oh that must still be completed. Just to make sure the message really has sunk in. Now leave Mr. Turner, while you still can."

"Yes, Miss. Bye."

I knew it would be pushing my luck to try get off the extra detention but I had to try didn't I? Never mind. Time to get home now. I walk again, but taking the long way today, opting not to take the shortcut through the distillery grounds, just peering in through the fence to see if there are any signs of anything having gone down there yesterday (Apart from my own KO moment obviously). But it looks as derelict and as forlorn as it always does. I suppose that is somewhat relieving but it doesn't completely alleviate all my worries. Just because it doesn't look like anything happened doesn't mean it didn't. Something might still have happened. And if not here it might have happened as Jack left the grounds of the factory. I need to find out if he is okay. There has to be some way...

I turn away from the fence and walk away, fast.

I know what I have to do.

I arrive home and take the stairs two at a time. I enter my room and dump my bag onto the floor. Picking up my laptop from where I left it this morning I kick off my shoes and sit on my bed, using the pillow behind me as a support for my back. I prise it open, press the power button and watch it flare into life. I type in my password and when the home screen shows up I immediately click on the browser icon. I bring up my Facebook page, go straight to the search bar and as I knew it would be, the most recent search is Jack's profile. I click into it and look for any sign of activity to confirm that Jack is okay. Nothing. No status updates for more than forty- eight hours. No likes. No shares. No nothing. No sign of him having been online at all since before the incident yesterday.

Fuck! If he hasn't even been online, there must be

something seriously wrong. Something must be preventing him from accessing his computer or phone. Broken hands maybe? Or maybe he is lying unconscious in a hospital bed. I slam the laptop closed and throw it to the end of my bed where it balances precariously for a minute, threatening to fall off and hit the floor. But it doesn't. I grab it just in time and place it back onto my desk, slamming it down harder than is necessary.

The rest of the night passes in a blur.

Only one thing on my mind.

Only one thing I care about right now.

Jack.

CHAPTER TEN

Sherlock Turner

I don't get much sleep, just a couple of hours, spending most of the time lying on my back, staring at the dark ceiling, thoughts of Jack swirling around my mind. So eventually, when the light starts to pour in through my window, I get up, get showered, dress in my uniform and head downstairs to the kitchen. I make myself a cup of tea and lean against the worktop, feeling a headache coming on. So I massage my temples, trying to alleviate the thumping. I search through the presses under the sink until I find some pain relief tablets then pop two into my mouth and take a big mouthful of tea, washing them down.

"I thought I heard someone down here."

I turn away from the worktop and see my mum, coming in through the kitchen door, still in her dressing gown and slippers. Her long brown hair is tied up in a bun, just a few wisps sticking up at odd angles. Looking up at the clock on the wall over the radiator I see it is still early. Only 7:00am.

"Yeah, I couldn't sleep. Sorry if I woke you."

"No, not at all sweetheart, I always wake up early. I have to. To make sure you're up for school."

"Cup of tea?" I ask her, already dropping a teabag into her favourite mug.

"Okay, what's wrong?" She folds her arm across her chest and glares at me.

"What do you mean?"

"Dean, I'm your mother, I can tell. You never sleep when you're troubled. Plus, you're drinking tea. Something you only ever do when you're upset."

Okay she's got me there. I do only ever make tea when I'm upset and need to think things over. It usually makes me feel better. I don't know what it is. Maybe the caffeine awakens something inside me. I usually pop the kettle on, have a chat with my mum, talk until I feel better. But this time is different. I can't tell my mum what's going on. Not all of it anyway. But I have to tell her something. Throw her off the scent. So I opt for the easy part. Something I can explain.

"I broke up with Karen."

"Oh, Dean, no. Are you okay Sweetheart?"

She takes a couple of hurried steps over to where I'm standing and wraps her arms around me. The soft warmness of her hug is comforting and I feel almost like a kid again. Hell, I feel almost normal again, even just for a brief moment. Like the past two days haven't happened. But I can't escape the fact that they have. There is no escaping from that. After a few more minutes of holding me tightly she grabs me by the shoulders, at arms length and looks into my eyes.

"Are you sure you're okay sweetheart? Breakups can be really difficult."

"Yeah, I'm fine Mum." She looks at me, clearly dubious. "Honestly," I add. "I'm fine. Things just didn't work out for us. Neither of us were really happy. But we're still going to be friends."

She pulls me into a hug again, this time almost squeezing the life out of me.

"Oh sweetheart."

She lets go and before she can grab hold of me again I pick up my cup of tea from the counter and drain the last few mouthfuls. I place it into the sink and head for the door.

"I'm, er, going to head into school early Mum. I need to see if Ja- ames, if, er, James turns up for school today." Damn it. Almost let Jack's name slip out. "He owes me a fiver from last week."

She looks at me across the kitchen, suspicion clearly growing. I am a right idiot. I don't even know anyone called James and she knows that. She looks as if she is going to say something but changes her mind and smiles.

"Okay sweetheart. Have a good day. And remember you can always talk to me you know."

"Yeah, er, thanks, you too Mum."

Relieved that she let that little slip up slide, probably thinking it's just a new friend or something, I run upstairs to my room. I grab my bag from the floor, take my PE gear out, throw it into the laundry basket at the top of the stairs and head back down, pausing only to shout a goodbye to my mum still in the kitchen and slip out into the cool autumn breeze where I start making my way to school. I walk slowly, taking my time, looking at all of the houses along the way. Drapes closed, blinds drawn, their inhabitants likely still snoozing peacefully in their beds.

Wait! I stop mid stride. Didn't Jack say the other day he only lived a few streets away from me? Yeah, he did. He definitely did. When we were walking together. I'm sure of it. But fuck, I have no way of knowing which one. I have never seen Jack around here. And there are lots of streets within walking distance of mine. That is a shit tonne of houses. And, even if I did know exactly which street, I would still be none the wiser as to which house it actually is that he lives in. I could end up knocking on every single door in the damn street. And that's not a task I want to undertake.

But now I know what I have to do. Time to do some investigating. With a new found determination in my stride, I make my way to school.

The school gates are still locked when I arrive outside. I pace up and down glancing at my watch every few minutes, waiting for someone to come along and open the gates. I sit down on the side of the footpath but stand up when I spot a familiar grey Toyota come trundling towards me. It comes to an abrupt stop just a few inches from the front of the gates and Mr. Danvers steps out. He looks at me with mild curiosity and I notice his slightly dishevelled appearance, the cuffs and collar of his shirt not buttoned up, his tie missing, his bald head glistening with sweat.

"Bit early this morning, Mr.Turner, school doesn't start for another forty-five minutes," he says, looking at his watch, then adding: "Not up to any further mischief I hope."

"No, not at all sir." I think, for a second, about asking whether he would be able to give me Jack's address. I could make up an excuse. Say that I have noticed how Jack hasn't been at school and that I'd like to bring him the homework that he missed. But that seems too odd and considering what happened on Monday, I don't imagine he will be in a very giving mood. Especially to me.

He will probably think I'm trying to cause more trouble. Better not risk it. "I, er, just want to get a jump start on my essay for Miss Perkins."

"Ah, excellent. Good lad. Always great to see our students invested in their studies and not causing any trouble." He raises his eyebrows at me and I give him a shaky smile and tilt of my head as I watch him undo the lock and chain from around the gates. He gestures towards the steps that lead to the main entrance, as he pulls the gates wide open, one at a time. "Wait for me by the door and I"ll let you into the library."

"Yes sir."

He slides back into the drivers seat of his car and drives slowly around to the right of the school grounds where any teacher that drives to school is permitted to park their car. I follow behind on foot, passing through the now open gates and walk up the concrete steps where I wait for Mr. Danvers to return. When he does, he is carrying a brown leather briefcase and is wearing a tie that he was not wearing a few minutes ago. The sweat that was on his forehead is all but gone and the cuffs of his shirt are buttoned around his wrists.

"Nice tie, sir."

"Oh, yes, thank you Mr. Turner." He pats it down and unlocks the front doors, swinging them open, the light from outside now illuminating the corridor. "Now, the library should be open already, but just in case it is not, here is the key," he says, handing me the bunch of keys he used to open the gates and doors a minute ago. "Which you are to bring back to me immediately when you see whether it is open or not. Understood? Immediately."

"Yes sir, of course" I say back, nodding and pocketing the bunch of keys. "They're safe with me."

I wasn't actually planning on going to the library but I have to now. But never mind, it might actually turn out to be useful. There might be something that will help me find out where Jack lives. A yearbook or something, maybe. Just something. Anything. Even an indication as to who might be able to tell me.

Walking through the deserted corridors by myself I can't help but suppress the shivers that run down my back. I don't know if you have ever been in an empty school by yourself but I can tell you it is just so fucking creepy. Deserted, dreary, downright eerie. It is amazing the difference even just a few students make to the overall atmosphere of the place.

I get to the library quicker than usual, partly because I was walking faster, not wanting to be alone in the eerie corridors and partly because I didn't have to force my way through groups of teenagers that usually block the way. I reach out and try the handle but the door is locked so I take the big bunch of keys out of my pocket and try to find the one for the library doors. Each key has a little different coloured plastic keyring attached to it, with writing on it saying which room it is for: Master Key, B17, B12, Boys Bathroom etcetera, etcetera, etcetera.

Finally, I find the one for the library and open the door. I step inside and lock the door behind me, leaving the key in the back of the door. Students and teachers are going to start arriving soon and I can't risk getting caught. I begin the hunt, searching for some old yearbooks but I can't find any. I need to think. Quick.

I spot the librarians desk over in the far corner. I run over and rifle through some of the pieces of paper that are scattered all over. Nothing. I fire up the computer sitting on top of the desk but it's password protected. Damn. I look down at my watch.

It is almost time for the first class of the day and I'm obviously not going to find anything here. I abandon my search and slip out into the corridor which now contains a handful of students mingling around, chatting, waiting for the first class to begin. What was I even thinking anyway? How was I supposed to find out where Jack lives in the *library*? As if that sort of stuff would be just left lying around in a book somewhere. Idiot.

When I reach Danvers' office, I raise my still bruised hand and rap lightly on the door. No answer. I try the handle and surprisingly it opens. I go inside but the room is empty. No doubt he is out shepherding the students into school, making sure that everyone is in on time and that their uniforms are up to standard. I suppose I can just leave the keys here. On his desk. I take them out of my pocket and walk around behind his desk and when I start to place them on the surface two things catch my eye. Firstly, there are two of the same coloured keyrings, each with the words Master Key written on them and secondly Mr. Danvers' computer is on, unlocked and with several files open on the screen. I look from the computer to the door of the office, several times. This has to be a dream. Right? After the rough couple of days I have had there is no way I could be this lucky. Right?

I look around and wait for a few seconds but it doesn't look like Mr. Danvers is going to be back any time soon. Now is my chance. I have to do it. Otherwise I will never be able to find out where Jack lives. I grab the mouse and click through a lot of folders until I reach one that says 'Student Records'. This is it. I click in and scroll down, spotting my own name as I'm scrolling but I don't stop to read it.

Eventually I reach Jack's record and read every word carefully. Woah! His grades are off the charts. I knew he was clever but this is like on another level. No. Stop snooping. I only need one thing. I scroll again and... success. I find the address, smile to myself. I know exactly where that is. I close down anything that was opened up and try to make the screen look exactly as it did before I started clicking around. There, I think that's it. I put the mouse back exactly in the spot I got it from and place the keys in the centre of the desk, the two keyrings that are same colour catching my eye again.

I can't, can I? I mean, I really shouldn't. But come on, when is a chance like this ever going to crop up again? Yeah, never, thats when. So I have to right? I slip it away from the rest of the keys on the bunch and place it in the breast pocket of my shirt, making sure it's not visible through my jumper and slip back out into the corridor, closing the door quietly as I do so, knowing that I look way, way more smug than I have any right to.

CHAPTER ELEVEN

House Call

My first few classes pass by without any major happenings. The fact that Jack doesn't turn up for the second day in a row only niggles at me a little bit and my breathing remains steady. Because I have his address now. I know what I am going to do. I am officially a man with a plan. But I can't believe how lucky my morning has been. I mean, come on, opportunities like that never crop up for me. I can't stop smiling to myself. But I don't want to dwell on it too much. Just have to hope my new found luck keeps up for the rest of the day. At least until I do what I have to do.

When the bell rings for lunch at the end of Miss Perkins' English class I pack up my notebook and things and head out into the corridor with the rest of my classmates. Instead of taking a left and heading down to the cafeteria with the rest of the school, I go right, head for the back stairs. I need to slip out undetected and I shouldn't run into anyone going this way. Everyone will be too busy trying to get a good spot on the queue before all the good food is gone and they are left with the soggy chips and dried up mash from the bottom of the scantily filled bain maries.

We are, technically, not actually allowed to leave school during lunch, which is a stupid rule if you ask me, as most of the older students actually do slip out to the shop. But I keep my eyes peeled for any teachers who may be on the prowl and I almost get to the back entrance before hearing something. Voices. Coming towards me. I backtrack a little, looking for somewhere I can slip into, to go unseen. It might be a couple of teachers.

I look to the door on my left. Yes! A store room. I pull the master key that I, ahem, borrowed earlier from my shirt pocket, unlock the door and slip inside. I close the door behind me and immediately I am plunged into total darkness. I lean up against the door, my hand resting gently on the handle, the side of my head pressed up against the hard wood. The voices are coming closer. I can't quite make out what they are saying but I recognise them. It's not teachers. It is Dave and Karen. Of course it bloody is. And as luck would bloody well have it they stop right outside the door. Great!

I can hear everything they are saying now. I silently urge them to pass on, holding my breath, staying completely still.

"Maybe I should text him, just to see how he is," I hear Karen say. There is some obvious concern in her voice. My heart is starting to beat fast in my chest.

"I wouldn't babe, just leave it." Dave this time.

"But we haven't seen him. Maybe he's skipping school. I just want to know that he's okay."

"Don't worry he's fine. And he's not skipping. I was talking to a guy who's in his English class just now who says he's been smiling into his book all morning.

"Really?" She sounds uncertain.

"Yeah, babe, honestly. So he's fine. We just need to give

him some space. To come to terms with it and that. He'll be back talking to us in no time."

"Okay. Come on then, I need to finish this Biology homework before lunch is over."

I listen as they move on, their footsteps fading away, going in the direction I came from a few minutes ago. I know I shouldn't have heard any of that but it is actually a good thing I did. It's clear that Karen is still concerned for my well being. And even Dave seems to be too. Yeah, he didn't say it out straight. And he won't either. He is not the type to go around expressing his feelings. But the fact that he has been asking about me from people in my class speaks volumes to me. The wanker really does care.

I smile to myself and head out of the dingy store room, pass by the lockers and sneak out the back door. I skirt around a bunch of overly relaxed looking guys and girls who are passing around a suspiciously large cigarette behind the bike sheds, heading out onto the main street and turn right, just as if I would if I was walking home. But I'm not going home. I am going to Jack's house. To see once and for all that he is okay. Stop me worrying every time I think about him. He is going to be fine. I have to believe that.

I reach the old distillery and slip in through the hole in the fence just like I did a couple of days ago, only alone this time. I make my way around the old building, its walls towering above me, the gravel under my feet making loud crunching noises that echo through the empty grounds. I look up at the building and notice how almost every single window that is set high up at the top of the building is broken, large holes right through their centres. No doubt broken by the yobs that frequent the grounds every evening.

I sidle my way out through the fence on the other side of the factory, opposite to the one I came in through and walk until I reach the beginning of the first set of houses in this part of the town. I slow down to consider which way would be best to go. Straight on would mean having to pass by my house and risk being spotted by my mum or by my dad, who might be home on his lunch break. So that is out of the equation straight away. Going left would mean walking by Dave Rudden's house. This carries a slightly smaller chance of being spotted but, still, his mum knows me quite well and would tell my mum if she caught me skipping school. So right it is, the long way around, meaning I will have to pass Rykers Field.

I walk quickly past the open field, occasionally glancing across it to make sure no-one has seen me. The worn out goal posts that were erected on the field years ago still stand upright (barely), though the nets that were once attached to them are long gone. I played football there many times when I was younger. Before girls (and now boys- well, just one boy) entered the scene. Before life took over and more adult endeavours attracted mine and my friend's hormone riddled attention.

Anyway I walk for a bit and stop when I reach the end (or the start, I'm not sure which direction the numbers go in) of the street I'm looking for. Hang on though, I have only just realised that I have absolutely no clue what to say when I get to Jack's house. I was so determined just to get here that I didn't give any thought to how odd it will be just showing up to his house in the middle of the school day. I think it is safe to assume that it is going to be AWKWARD. But fuck it, I will just wing it. The best outcomes often come from people just winging things.

I look up at the number of the first house to my left.

Number Four. So this at the start of the street. The file on Mr. Danvers' computer said Jack lives at number Twenty Seven. Judging by the length of the street that should be about a quarter of the way along, so I start walking, looking carefully at the wooden number plates screwed into the walls beside each door. Eventually the house I'm looking for comes into view.

It is not what I as expecting, at all. Looks like the outside walls haven't been painted in a long time, maybe decades. And I can see that the window sills and surrounds were once white but are now covered in moss and dirt. Weeds are growing up at each corner of the garden where the surrounding, low brick walls meet the concrete of the driveway. This can't be Jack's house can it? Maybe the files on Mr. Danvers' computer are out of date. I look around at the houses to the left and right of it. They are in a a similar state of disrepair but not quite as bad as this one. I guess there is only one way to find out. I reach out and push open the small metal gate in front of me, the rusted hinges squeaking faintly as it swings inward.

It is a short walk up the concrete driveway, to the faded and weather beaten, but clearly mahogany coloured front door. There is no doorbell or door knocker, so I reach out and use the letter box as a knocker, the clang echoing loudly through the still air around me. There is a sound of movement on the other side of the door. So someone is definitely home. A shadow passes close to the little frosted window set into the door. It opens slowly and a woman answers. Jack's mum, maybe. She's younger than mine. Early to mid thirties at most. She must have had Jack when she was pretty young. Her hair is tied up in a messy bun that is skewed sideways on top of her head. She is thin, slight bags and dark circles under her eyes, but she is not sickly looking if you know what I mean. She just looks normal.

"Hi, er, Mrs. Hawkins?" I ask (politely of course).

She looks me up and down, clearly noticing that I'm from the same school as Jack. (The uniform obviously gives that away). Her eyes linger for a second on my bruised knuckles and she pulls the door closed a little.

"Yes?"

Good, I have the right house. Thank fuck!

"Is, er, Jack in?"

She doesn't answer immediately and my heart starts to beat really fast. Tell me he's here. Please. She narrows her eyes at me. "Yeah, he is." Oh, thank fuck! He's here! I nearly sink to my knees, relief coursing through my entire body. "But he's not well." No, no, what do you mean he's not well? Don't say that. He has to be.

"He's not hurt is he?," I say, my voice sounding very wheezy.

"No? He just has a stomach bug." She looks at me suspiciously.

Stupid, I shouldn't have asked if he was hurt. Bruised knuckles plus me asking if he's hurt. Bad idea. Now she knows something is up.

"Who did you say you were?" she asks me.

"Oh, I'm sorry, I'm Dean. Dean Turner. A friend of Jack's. Fom school." I pull at the end of my jumper but I must look like an idiot because she's already noticed the uniform.

"Dean?"

"Yes, Mrs. Hawkins. Dean Turner. I live a few streets away." I gesture over my shoulder with my thumb. "I'm in the same class as Jack."

"Jack has never mentioned a friend from school called

Dean."

Well, of course he hasn't. But I try to look a little confused. Like we've been friends for years and she should know who I am. "Oh really? That's odd."

"Yeah. So how can I help you, Dean?"

Shit, I should have planned this better. Should have thought about what I was going to say. Er...Er... Homework. Yes, the excuse I was going to use on Danvers this morning. Should work. Hopefully.

"I just, er, wanted to bring Jack the homework he missed out on, seeing as he wasn't in school and that."

Her shoulders relax a little. "Oh, well that's kind of you. Thank you. I'll give it to him later."

Wait, what? She half raises her hand, expecting me to hand it over. No, I have to see him you stupid woman.

"Would it be possible that I could give it to him myself? Only there's a question that the teacher asked me to explain to him personally. Just to make sure he fully understands what he has to do."

"Oh, um, okay. You better come in then, Dean."

"Thank you, Mrs. Hawkins. It won't take long. I have to be back at school soon anyway."

She moves to the side and gestures for me to enter. "Just through that door there," she says, pointing to the door on the left.

I noticed it as soon as I entered the hallway, but when I walk into the living room it becomes even more apparent. The difference between the outside appearance and the inside appearance of the house is incredible. It is like two completely different houses. Inside, everything is spotless, clean, nice neutral coloured walls, not a speck of dust on the hardwood floors. Nothing seems to be out of place, even down to the television remote controls that are lined up in what looks like order of size on the mantlepiece.

"Why don't you take a seat Dean, I'll just go and get Jack."

I sit down on the edge of the clean, brown leather sofa, removing my bag from my back and placing it at my feet as Mrs. Hawkins leaves, via the door we came in through. I hear her footsteps ascending the stairs, quickly, followed by her muffled voice, though I can't make out what she's saying exactly. There's a muffled response and my heart gives a little jolt. It's Jack.

There is a bit of back and forth between the two voices, each one sounding equally confused. I stare at the door for a long time and eventually I hear two sets of feet come padding down the stairs, the first rather hurried, the other more calmly. The door opens inward, gently and Mrs. Hawkins re-enters the room, closely followed by Jack.

I want to smile at him. Show him everything is okay. That I care. But I can't. My whole body has gone rigid. I try to speak but my tounge feels heavy, my teeth clenched together. Jack stands by the window, his arms folded in front of his chest. Mrs. Hawkins looks at me suspiciously. She looks at Jack, as if waiting for his instructions, as if waiting on Jack to confirm that I'm not some nutter. His lips raise slightly at the sides and he tilts his head forward.

"Okay, I'll leave you two boys alone then shall, I? But not too long, mind you. You should be in bed resting." Mrs. Hawkins says, looking at Jack, her eyes lingering on her son's face. Searching. The way my mum does to me.

"I know Mum, this will only take a minute."

"Okay, I'll just be in the kitchen." She leaves through

the door once again, this time closing it fully, the latch clicking firmly into place. I listen as her footsteps retreat down the hallway. A faint clink of crockery permeating through the walls a second later means she must be making herself some tea. How very typical.

I look over at Jack, who is still staring at me, his arms folded across his chest, his back to the window. The light shimmers around him.he looks so good, wearing a pair of navy blue shorts, his tanned legs exposed, the curly, black hairs almost glistening in the light. The white t-shirt he has on is clinging to his body. His slim, muscular body. No longer hidden by the oversized uniform I'm so used to seeing him in. I feel my body relax, the sides of my mouth beginning to rise and I realise now, looking at him, how much I want to touch him. Kiss him. Taste hi-

"What are you doing here?" His question is direct. His tone harsh.

"You haven't been to school."

"And?"

"I just needed to know that you're okay."

"Why wouldn't I be?"

"I thought something might have happened to you. After I left you at the distillery by yourself the other night. And when you didn't turn up for school I thought you were hurt. That Jimmy Browne might have attacked you or something." I push my hands together on my lap, my fingers interlocking, my palms sweating against each other.

"He didn't. I came straight home. But why would you care anyway?"

"I don't know. I just haven't been able to stop thinking about it. About you."

"You're only trying to protect yourself."

"What? How?" I stand up, move closer to him, my hands coming apart, my bag tipping over onto its side as my feet brush against it. He drops his hands to his sides and moves his feet into a more stable position. The tension between us feels thick in the air.

"You just want to make sure I haven't told anyone that you attacked me."

"Attacked you?" The words come out louder than I intended, so I lower my voice to barely more than a whisper. "I didn't attack you! I was stopping you from kissing me!"

"I saw the way you looked at me. You wanted it."

"That's not true. I had a girlfriend. I didn't want it."

"Yeah? Then why do you have that same look in your eyes now?"

I turn away from him, my head directed towards the floor. I rub my temples with my thumb and index finger, thoughts swirling like crazy through my mind.

"Look," I say, turning back around to face him. "I'm not here trying to protect myself, I just wanted to make sure you were okay. I was worried."

He takes half a step closer to me. I can see his plump, red lips, his piercing blue eyes.

"Really?"

"Yes. And I'm sorry I hit you. I dunno why I did it. I was just surprised and confused and, I dunno, but I am really sorry."

We stare at each other for what feels like an eternity, silent words passing back and forth between us. He has relaxed, his defensive stance no longer in place. I don't know about him, but I want to say more, tell him how I feel or how I think I feel. Or at least just how I've been feeling the past few days. But I can't. Not yet anyway. I'm not ready to say it out loud. Saying it out loud makes it too real. Too concrete. But he knows, he said it himself, the way I am looking at him. He can see it in my eyes. And I can see it in his eyes too. He tried to kiss me for a reason. And it felt right for a reason.

Eventually, after a while of surveying me, he speaks. "My mum said something about you having brought the homework I missed out on."

That is not what I was expecting him to say at all.

"Oh." I laugh to myself a little. "I don't have any sorry. I just said that so I could see you."

"Now that, that is just cheeky," he says, smiling.

"Just a bit."

We smile at each other.

"You're not really sick are you?" I ask, looking for signs of illness, obviously failing to see any. So much for that stomach bug his mum said he has.

"Er, no. I was just trying to avoid you to be honest. But I didn't know you were worried about me." He bats his eyelids at me and pouts his lips.

"Yeah, yeah, don't flatter yourself Hawkins. So will you come back to school tomorrow?"

"I'll think about it. As long as you don't punch me again."

"I can't make those sort of promises," I say, flashing him my infamous, cheesy smile. "Especially if you keep making that stupid duck face at me."

"You better get used to it, Dean Turner."

Smiling, I look down at my watch, relishing the way he just used my full name. I watch the little hand move slowly around. I've been here too long. I am going to be late back to school. And I can't risk getting any more detention. I have enough of that to be getting through.

"I have to go," I say to Jack, picking up my bag from the floor beside the sofa and flinging it up onto my shoulder. "Please, come back to school. It's not the same when you're not there, you know, being a know it all, answering every single question."

He opens the door to the hallway and slips out, his footsteps light on the floor. I am hot on his heels, my footsteps considerably more heavy. When we are both fully in the hallway he stands by the front door, his hand resting on the brass handle. I move closer to him, reach my hand up, placing it on top of his. His skin feels like magic under my fingertips. So warm, so soft. He leans in close to me, his scent wafting towards me, infiltrating my senses. So clean. So fresh. I inhale deeply, lift my other hand and place it on his hip. I move my head towards his, inching closer to his plump, red lips, wanting it this time, wanting to feel his lips on mine, ready to ta-

Tcht!

The noise of a door opening followed by footsteps at the end of the hallway makes me jump. I straighten up, moving away from Jack. His mum is standing there, a tea towel in her left hand, a clean mug in the other, eyebrows raised, a knowing look on her face.

"Leaving Dean?"

"Yes Mrs. Hawkins. I have to be getting back to school. And thank you for inviting me into your home. It's lovely."

"That's very nice of you to say. Thank you Dean."

Jack opens the door and I step out into the driveway. The cool air hits me hard but it feels refreshing on my face. I didn't realise how hot I had gotten inside the house. But now, outside in the fresh air, I can feel the sweat under my armpits, the heat radiating from my cheeks. I walk forward a few paces and look back. Jack is standing in the open doorway, smiling.

"See you at school," he says and shuts the door. I can see his dark silhouette through the little window. Standing there. Still. Unmoving.

"Yeah," I say to myself, half smiling, half laughing, definitely happy. "See you at school."

CHAPTER TWELVE

Kissing

Thursday. 8:00 am. In the bathroom. I place my toothbrush back in the holder and turn off the cold tap, halting the flow of water. I raise my head and look into the mirror. My hair is getting long, starting to flop down into my eyes A haircut is definitely due soon. I brush it back with my hand and examine myself closely. I look somewhat refreshed. Better than I have all week. Probably because I actually slept well last night. I wasn't fretting about anything. I was able to just relax, happy knowing that Jack is okay. Happy knowing that he will be coming back to school today.

It was true what I said to him yesterday. It was actually not the same with him not being there. I guess the old cliche is true after all. It is only when someone is gone that you realise how much they are missed. And now that I actually think about it, the classroom really did feel empty without Jack there, answering all the teachers questions. But at least that will be back to normal today. Jack will be back, showing off just how smart he is.

But I don't really know how I'm supposed to behave around Jack now. Do we talk to each other? Or do we just go back to normal, smiling at each other as we pass in the hallways? I don't know. But it's not like we can pretend that nothing happened between us. There is obviously something there. He clearly likes me and I think I like him too. It is just that I have never done anything like this before. I have never even thought about doing anything like this. But every time I think about Jack and how he kissed me and how, for the briefest moment that I let it happen, it felt good, felt natural, I feel happy.

But it feels strange too, very confusing. It is something we will have to explore, I suppose. But it's not like we can just go about doing it in public. I don't want people to know what happened. It cannot become public knowledge. At least not yet anyway. But maybe I shouldn't dwell on it too much. I just have to let things unfold naturally.

"For God's sake Dean! Open this door!"

I wipe my hands quickly on the towel hanging on the rail beside me and open the door. My mum is standing in the hallway just outside the bathroom, looking furious.

"What's wrong?"

"What's wrong? What's wrong? I've been calling you for ten bloody minutes, that's what's wrong! Why didn't you answer me?"

"Oh. I didn't hear you. Sorry Mum."

"Don't apologise to me, just get your arse off to school or you'll be late. And start bloody listening Dean."

"I will Mum. I just got lost in my thoughts. I was just thinking about what a wonderful mother I have."

I lean in and give her a quick peck on the cheek. Her lips start to curl up at the sides, but she stops herself from breaking into a smile. She starts pulling her dressing gown in tighter against her body.

"Right, well, go to school. Now, you little git."

I grab my stuff from my room and head out into the sunshine, walking fast, the sun warm on my back, my shadow slinking along in front of me, elongated and distorted on the worn concrete.

I get to school just as the bell is ringing for the first class. I manage to slip into the room and into my usual seat at the side of the room just a few seconds before Mr. Walsh arrives, shuts the door and without missing a beat, starts to take the attendance. A quick glance up to the front makes my chest tighten and my palms begin to sweat. No, no, no. That can't be right. The seat Jack usually sits in is empty. Why has he not turned up? I was sure he would. I thought I had fixed everything. I really thought he would be here today. I can't believe he didn't show.

As I wipe the palms of my hands dry on the navy fabric of my trousers and and take a deep breath to try to control my heartbeat and think of what to do next, there is a knock on the door and, without looking up from the attendance book, Mr. Walsh calls out.

"Come in."

"Sorry I'm late sir. I was with Mr. Danvers"

My brain register's the voice before what I'm seeing comes into focus.

It's Jack.

He hands Mr. Walsh a piece of paper, which the squat teacher takes a moment to read, before nodding his head and gesturing towards the empty seat at the front of the class that, just moments ago, caused me to enter panic mode.

"No problem Mr. Hawkins. Take a seat, we're just getting started."

I lean forward in my seat a little, bringing my elbows

to rest on the much graffitied wooden desk top as Jack takes his seat at the front of the room close to Mr. Walsh As he places his bag on the ground beside him he twists his head around, looks at me and smiles. That wonderful, perfect smile. I smile back, my body relaxing, no longer taut with panic.

And that is how the rest of the day passes by, Jack and myself exchanging smiles, back and forth through each class that we share together. They are all mostly in the morning though, my smile disappearing completely by my last class when ten minutes into it dawns on me that I have detention again this afternoon after school.

The bell rings at three thirty and I exit the classroom I'm in and start making my way to today's assigned detention room. I turn the corner and see Jack standing outside, his hands by his sides, his head inclined towards the wall. I make my way up to him and stand near him. I clear my throat to get his attention but he doesn't look up, probably thinking I'm just some random kid that also has detention. So I move closer to him.

"Hey."

He raises his head and smiles at me. A weird sensation bubbles up in my stomach. I'm not sure if I am just getting hungry or if it's something more. Either way, it doesn't matter. Just knowing that he is smiling at me makes the thought of this afternoons detention seem almost bearable. I turn around, placing my back against the wall and Jack does the same, the two of us now side by side, the backs of our hands touching. I rub the back of his hand gently with my my fingers, feeling the warmth of his skin against mine. I turn my head towards him.

He opens his mouth and starts to say something but trails off into silence, looking past me to the end of the corridor. I turn my head and see Jimmy Browne making his way towards us and suddenly I realise how close Jack and I are standing, our fingers starting to intertwine. I try to move away without drawing attention to us but Jimmy must notice because, when he reaches us, he pushes Jack out of the way.

"Don't get too close to that faggot, Turner, people will start thinking you're one of them."

I look past Jimmy, to where Jack has started to move away, stuffing his hands into his pockets, his head now directed firmly at the ground. Immediately I tense up, my hands twitching, my eyebrows meeting in the middle of my face.

"Yeah? And what would one of them be then?" I ask him, taking a deep breath, readying myself for what I know is bound to happen for standing up to Jimmy Browne.

"What?"

He looks taken aback. He was expecting me to play along. But that is definitely not going to happen. There is no way am I letting this prick make Jack feel like shit. No way.

"Deaf as well as completely fucking stupid now are you?"

"What did you just say to me Turner? You better be fucking messing." I see his hand ball into a fist and a look of anger fall cross his face. "Tell me you're fucking messing Turner. Because I'd hate to have to kick the shit out of you in front of this poof."

I don't say anything, balling my own hand into a fist instead. I look to Jack who is no longer looking at the ground but has his gazed trained on me and Jimmy, our noses and chests just centimetres apart now.

I risk another glance over at Jack, hoping that Jimmy doesn't strike now while my eyes are averted. I make eye contact with him, expecting to see encouragement on Jack's face, to see him egg me on to punch Jimmy square in the mouth. But instead he is shaking his head furiously from side to side. I take a breath and realisation kicks in that he is probably right. It is so not worth making an enemy of Jimmy Browne. He has too many cronies willing to do anything he asks. Dangerous cronies. So, backing down, I uncurl my fists and force a smile onto my face, the muscles straining to keep it in place, fighting against the urge to turn into a scowl.

"Of course I'm joking Jimmy. You should have seen the look on your face though. Fucking priceless man!"

I see him searching my face, his beady eyes prying over my strained smile, trying to comprehend in his tiny, little fucktard brain what has just happened.

"You're just joking?"

"Uh-huh, of course. Just having a laugh Jimmy. Didn't mean anything by it."

"Right well I'll let it slide this time Turner, only 'cause I don't wanna be getting any more detentions if a teacher was to walk by and catch me beating the shit out of you. But just remember, I don't like being made a fool out of. Right?"

"Yeah no problem Jimmy, won't happen again. I was only having a joke. Stupid."

"Right."

The clip clop sound of high heels coming around the corner forces us fully back to our senses. Jack is practically glued to the wall by the door, eager to get out of this situation. I shove my hands into my pockets trying to look as nonchalant as possible and Jimmy, still looking perplexed at what just happened, doesn't take his eyes off me.

"Good afternoon gentlemen."

Miss Constance. Again. She must be on detention supervision all week. Usually the teachers rotate it every few days but she must be covering this entire week. That's a bit of a relief actually. Jimmy won't try anything with her here. If it was any other teacher I would be somewhat apprehensive about going into such a confined space with Jimmy Browne. But I know he won't try anything in front of Corporal Constance. It will be safe for the next hour at least.

"I said Good Afternoon, gentlemen."

"Good afternoon Miss," the three of us echo back in unison.

"In you go," she says, unlocking the door and swinging it open to stand aside and let us pass. Jack is the first to enter the room, followed by Jimmy and then me, at the rear of the trio. Jack heads straight for a desk at the top of the room while Jimmy heads straight for one at the back. Standard.

I watch as they do this, hesitating for a moment. I want to sit close to Jack, to be with him, as far away from Jimmy Browne as is physically possible in such a small room. But I can't. It would be too suspicious. I never sit at the front. And after Jimmy saw me and Jack standing so close outside, if I was to sit beside him now, he would definitely know something is going on. He might be thick as pig shit, but he could definitely work that out at least. Unfortunately.

So I turn and take a seat at the side of the classroom, slinging my bag down onto the floor. Jack turns around in his seat to look at me and I give him an apologetic look, casting my eyes to the side, in the direction of Jimmy, to indicate that I would be sitting with him if not for the brute sitting behind us. He gives a small nod of understanding before turning around in his seat and beginning to write.

I take out my own notebook and start writing, glancing at the clock at the top of the room over the Corporal's head occasionally, willing the hands to move faster, eager for this detention to end.

Eventually I stop writing, having exhausted my brain's capacity for any more work today and stuff everything back into my bag and wait for the two hands to come together on the clock. Almost like a machine on a timer, when the two hands of the clock do come together, meeting at the hour, Corporal Constance rises from her chair.

"That is all for today, gentlemen. You may leave. Except you please, Mr. Hawkins. I require a quick word with you."

Scooping my bag up from the floor beside me, I head for the door and out into the corridor. I make it almost to the main entrance before sensing a presence behind me. I turn around expecting it to be Jack, catching up to me, but my stomach hits the floor when I see that it is Jimmy. I turn back around, put my head down and keep walking, out into the grounds, all the while keeping on high alert, in case Jimmy pounces on me from behind. But he does nothing, just continues walking behind me. Following? Stalking? Only one way to find out.

I stop dead in my tracks and turn to face him. But he does nothing except keep walking, staring intensely at me as he passes me by, though remaining tight lipped. A small surge of relief courses through my body at the realisation that he is not going to do anything. Thank fuck. There is no way I would come away as the champion of a fight between me and that thug.

I take a deep breath in and the feeling of relief turns to elation at the sight of Jack coming down the stone steps outside the main entrance. He walks towards me.

"Hey."

"Hi."

"You came in today then?"

"I did."

"Good. Good. I'm, er, glad."

We stand there for a moment, looking at each other, not sure what to do. I stuff my hands into my pockets and take a few steps towards the open gate, looking back at Jack. "Wanna walk home with me?"

"Sure."

We turn right as we exit the school grounds, walking side by side.

"So what did the Corporal want?"

"Who?"

"Miss Constance."

"Oh. Nothing really. Just wanted to see if I was okay."

"And are you?"

"Am I what?"

"Okay?"

"Yeah of course. Worried about me are you?"

"Yeah, you wish."

We share a sensuous look and continue on our way, together, until we reach the old distillery and I let Jack pass through the gap in the railings first. He walks a little ahead of me this time, giving me a chance to watch him as he walks in front of me.

"Keep your fists to yourself," he says, finally turning

around to face me, referencing the last time the both of us walked through here together.

"I'll try," I say, shooting him a wink, the both of us now smirking at each other.

We come to a halt close to the spot where I hit Jack the last time. We look around at the empty grounds, the desolate building to our left towering above us.

"Come here," I say, heading over to the side of the building. I sit down on the dusty ground, the gravel still warm from the day's sun beaming down on it, the cold of the evening not yet set in. I press my back up against the wall, and drag my knees up in front of my chest. "Sit."

He looks at me, then at the ground, clearly trying to decide if I'm being serious or not. I gesture towards the ground beside me. "Don't worry about the dirt. Just sit."

He lowers himself down onto the ground, adopting the same position I have, with his knees drawn up to his chest, his hands coming to rest on his thighs. We sit like this for ages, in silence, looking at each other occasionally. It's weird, but the silence between us is not uncomfortable. It is like we don't even need to say anything. We are happy just being in each other's company. Happy just being close to each other.

But as I study Jack's profile in the failing light, thinking about everything that has transpired over the last week, a question comes into my mind that has to be asked.

"Why do you let people like Jimmy treat you the way they do?"

Jack looks at me and a strange shadow seems to cross his face, his features distorting. But he looks away again before I have time to discern exactly what that expression is.

"No reason."

"What do you mean no reason? There has to be a reason. I've seen your abs, how fit you are. You could beat the shit out of assholes like Jimmy Browne any day."

"You've seen my abs?" He looks at me again, a look of confusion now taking up residence on his face. Shit. He doesn't know that. He doesn't know that I saw his Facebook pictures. I can try to lie but there's no point. I should just be honest.

"Yeah, I er, I saw them on your Facebook page."

"Oh, I didn't think people actually looked at that. Well anyone apart from my family."

He doesn't say anything after that, so I press on with my enquiry, eager to know the answer, watching his face carefully. "So why do you let little pricks like that pick on you?"

"I don't wanna talk about it. Not yet."

His features distort again, that shadow crossing his face, making him look unpleasant.

"Okay. Sorry."

I don't push for any more. I can see the emotion in his eyes, tears starting to well up in the corners. Something big must have happened. Something that instills real fear in him. And he said 'not yet'. Not yet is promising. Not yet means he will tell me at some stage. Just not right now. We fall back into a comfortable silence and I expect it to last for ages but it's broken by Jack.

"So you've been stalking my Facebook page," he says, rasing his eyebrow at me, a slight smile crossing his face.

"Er, no," I splutter. "Where on earth did you get that idea?"

"Yes you have."

I knock my knee against his, deliberately, playfully. "Shut up. It wasn't stalking. I was just looking for signs of activity. I thought you were dead"

"Yet you didn't think to send a friend request? A message?"

"I wasn't thinking straight."

"Yeah clearly." He smiles. This time I notice the small dimples that appear at the corner of his mouth when he does. "But you obviously liked what you saw."

"It, er, it was alright." I feel heat beginning to rise in my cheeks. "But where do you get off having abs like that?" I ask, raising my eyebrow at him this time.

"I do not."

"You do so."

He turns his head to look me fully in the eyes, his eyes glistening, his lips looking more inviting than ever. "Kiss me."

"What?"

"Kiss me."

"No," I say, laughing. He can't be serious. Not out here like this. Exposed. What if someone was watching?

"Fine." He turns away from me, looking dejected. "What are we doing here then? I thought you wanted it? But if you won't even..." He starts to get up.

I reach out and grab his arm, pulling him back down into his seated position. "I do. You know... I do. It's just... Not here. What if someone sees?"

"So what if someone sees?"

"So what? How can you say so what? You of all people should know what would happen if anyone saw us."

"Fine. If you're that embarrassed then I might as well just leave." He starts to get up again, pushin himself forward into a standing position.

"No. Don't. Don't leave. Please."

I look around me, scanning our surroundings carefully. No one is watching. There is no one near the fence, no one on either side of the street outside the grounds. I pull him close, reach my hand up and touch the soft flesh of his cheek and go for it. Forcefully. Passionately. I feel his hands make their way around my body, one coming to rest on my lower back, the other at the back of my head. His touch is soft, warm, comforting. Like nothing I've ever felt before.

I have kissed a few people in my seventeen years but none of them have ever compared to this. Not even my most passionate kisses with Karen were like this. This is different. This is just... I don't even know how to explain it. It just feels so right. So natural.

I don't know how much time passes, how long we spend in this embrace, our tongues sliding around as if independent from our bodies. Eventually we break apart and I lean my head back against the wall of the distillery.

I reach up and run my hand through my hair, my body tingling in places I didn't even know *could* tingle.

"Well that was....wow," I say.

"Yeah, yeah it was," Jack replies, his voice barely audible, his tongue slowly gliding across he surface of his lips.

Jack rests his head against my shoulder and we stay seated on the ground, watching as the sun sets and the street lights flicker into life. A soft buzzing sound makes Jack jump to his feet and pull his phone out of his pocket.

"Crap, that's my mum. I have to go. I should have been home ages ago."

I get to my own feet and only just have a chance to steady myself before Jack has grabbed the front of my shirt and is pressing his lips against mine.

"See you later," he says, breaking away from me and

running off, leaving me standing on my own.

I smooth down the front of my shirt, adjust my trousers, pushing everything back into place and head out through the broken railings, into the street.

Something flashes by, in the corner of my eye, like a shadow moving in the distance. I stop and squint my eyes but I can't see anything. It's too dark. Besides, it's probably nothing, there was no one around. Probably just a stray cat. Or a fox or something. Out scavenging for food. So I carry on, heading home, pushing it out of my mind.

It doesn't take long to get home and when I do I exchange the usual pleasantries with my mum and dad over the dinner table, watch TV for a while afterwards, not really taking anything in, content with just replaying today's events over in my head. Eventually I decide to head upstairs. I will have a shower, maybe do some homework etcetera, etcetera.

I feel my phone vibrate in my pocket as I get to my bedroom. I pull it out and look at the screen.

It is a Facebook friend request from Jack.

I click accept.

Obviously.

CHAPTER THIRTEEN

Just A Teenage Dream

Friday morning. I'm at school. Mr. Danvers has gathered my entire year in the assembly hall. I stifle a yawn. I didn't get much sleep last night, spending most of it messaging Jack, as well as doing some other stuff that I'd rather not divulge the details of. Least of all to you. All I will say is that it was very, er, pleasant. Yes. Very pleasant indeed.

But for all the messaging we did last night, I still have no idea who Jack Hawkins really is. Every time I tried to get personal, find out about him, his life, what he likes and doesn't like, he would evade the topic, steer the conversation in another direction. And I want to get to know him. He is just so difficult.

But anyway, Mr. Danvers is telling us, in his most authoritative voice, that he has gathered us all here for not just one, but two surprise guest speakers. They want to talk to us about our future, our college options, what we want to do after school, all that sort of stuff. Pretty boring if you ask me. And woefully premature in my humble opinion. We still have eighteen months left before we even finish school. But according to good old Mr. Danvers "It is never too early to start planning for the future."

Loves to make plans for the future, does Mr. Danvers. He has probably had his funeral planned since he was ten. But that's not how I like to operate. I never like to plan anything too far in advance. I'd rather just go with the flow and see where it takes me.

I look around at the people sitting in the assembly hall, Dave and Karen sitting on the right hand side of the room, together, my other friend Luke sitting in the row behind. He sees me looking at him and gives a smile and a nod. I smile and nod back, then, turning my gaze away, I look to the front of the room where Jack is sitting, in the second row from the front, leant forward slightly, listening intently to everything Mr. Danvers is saying. I bet this is right up his street. And good for him, I suppose. If anyone from this whole year is going to amount to anything in the future it is Jack Hawkins.

I stifle another yawn and turn my attention back to the woman who has taken to the front of the assembly and is speaking now, her voice low and melodic, like a lullaby. It's hard to concentrate on what she's saying, she seems to be speaking in slow motion, dragging out every word for as long as she possibly can. I blink several times, my eyes becoming increasingly heavier, trying to stay focussed, to at least show some respect for the woman who has made time to come and....

A nudge to the side of my ribs jolts me to attention. I turn my head and I'm surprised to see Karen sitting in the chair beside me, smiling. Which is strange. I didn't realise she had swapped seats and didn't even hear the movement of her sitting down beside me.

"Hey, Karen what's up?" I say, in a whisper, keeping my voice down so as not to disturb the guest speaker or anyone nearby.

She doesn't say anything back, just continues smiling and reaches out her hand, placing it on my face. She leans her head towards me and places her lips on mine. I pull away from her and look around me but no one has noticed, everyone's eyes still trained in the speaker up front.

"What are you doing? Have you forgotten something?"

"Just kiss me," she says.

"No, not here. We're in school. And, Karen, we're not together anymore."

"I don't care, I just want to kiss you."

She starts to lean in again and I try to pull away but my body is rigid, my arms suddenly incapable of moving from my sides. What the fuck is happening to me? Why can't I move? Is this what it feels like to have a stroke? She stands up and throws her right leg over both of mine, sitting herself down on my lap, her skirt bunching up over her thighs. I blink again, trying to comprehend what the fuck is happening. Has she gone fucking insane? Or have I? Is this some sort of hallucination?

She throws her head forward, covering my face with her long hair. She starts whispering in my ear but it sounds strange, not like her at all. It is too deep, more like a guys voice.

"Karen, what the fuck is happening? You're really freaking me out. Stop it," I say, louder this time trying to get someone to look at us and put a stop to whatever the hell she is doing to me.

"I can't stop. I know you want it," she says, moving her head back into view. Only it's not her face at all. It is Jack's. Jack's face on Karen's body. And that was Jack's voice whispering in my ear. Now I know I am having some sort of psychotic break. But I still can't fucking move. Jesus, why can I not fucking move!

The Jack/Karen hybrid starts grinding on my lap. And it feels good. But I don't want it. Not now, not here. Not in front of everyone. I close my eyes, trying to block out what is happening but I can feel myself starting to harden, the blood rushing below my waist.

It is quite arousing but at the same time it is so fucking weird. 'It' (the Jack/Karen Hybrid) leans back a little and brings its hand down to where my flies are and starts to undo them. The hand reaches in and starts to touch me, gently stroking my now fully hard-

A loud noise makes me jump and my eyes spring open. The Jack/Karen hybrid is no longer on top of me. I must have fallen asleep. I sit up straight in my seat. Everyone around me is applauding. I join in, just as it is dying down and Mr. Danvers rises from his seat at the top of the room, offering his thanks to the two guest speakers.

When he is finished talking, reiterating the importance of what the two guests have just spoken about, he dismisses us and I start to stand in unison with the rest of the congregation of students. But I feel something pressed hard against my inner thigh. Fuck, the dream must have really turned me on because I'm still hard. I can see the outline of it through my trousers, squashed up against my leg. I sit back down and bend forward, pretending to tie the laces on my shoes, waiting for it to go flaccid again. When it is sufficiently soft, so as not to create too noticeable a bulge, I stand up and join the throng of students exiting the hall.

I walk through the doors and turn left, intending to head towards the classroom I should be in, my thoughts on the stange dream I just had, but I stop in my tracks when I hear a familiar laugh in the corridor ahead of me. I start to turn back to avoid them but Dave spots me and raises his hand slightly in a wave of acknowledgement. I can't turn my back on them now, or else they will think I am deliberately trying to avoid them. Which I'm not really, I just don't really have anything to say to Dave and Karen at the moment.

So bracing myself for any awkwardness that may ensue, I continue forward, walking directly towards them stopping when I catch up to them, the awkwardness already bubbling up slowly between us. But we are going to have to get past that awkward shit. We can't go on avoiding each other forever. We still have a lot of time left at this school together. Chances are I am going to see them every day. And Dave is my oldest and best friend in the world. It would be good to be back on regular terms with him. And with Karen of course.

"Hey, whats up?" I say, trying to sound as normal as possible, and to spare them the anguish of having to be the first ones to speak. "You guys been up to much?"

"Er, no not really," Dave says. "Just been taking things easy. You been okay?"

"Yeah, I've been great."

"Yeah, I bet you have," Karen says, almost under her breath, before I have a chance to say anything else. Her eyes widen in surprise as if she hadn't meant to say anything out loud. She looks away from me and starts to walk away. "I, er, need to go, I'm gonna be late for class."

"No wait, what's that supposed to mean?" I ask, taking a step towards her.

"Nothing," she says, reaching up and tugging at her hair. Her tell tale sign that she is hiding something. I look back to Dave, who has squinted his eyes- his tell tale sign of confusion.

Dave and I both start to say something but she cuts us off. "I didn't mean anything Dean, I promise. And I have to get to class, so see you later." She looks at me weirdly and speeds off, leaving me and Dave standing together in the corridor as other people pass by us.

So she says it was nothing but she is obviously hiding something. But what? She can't know about me and Jack, surely. I mean, how could she? The few times I've been alone with Jack, we've been just that: alone, there has been no one else around. So it can't be that, but it is definitely something. The way she said *"Yeah, I bet you have"* And the look she gave me as she sped away. I should probably try to find out what she knows. Before she tells anyone else. But would she even tell anyone else? I mean whatever it is she seems to know, she didn't even tell Dave. He was just as confused as I was.

I look back at Dave, who smiles at me. "Do you know what that was about?" I ask, just trying to initiate conversation more than anything else, because I already know he doesn't, his earlier look of confusion confirming that.

"No, not at all man. Weird as fuck,"

We start to laugh and before I can stop myself I pull my best friend into a one armed embrace. A manly embrace you might say. After a few seconds I let go.

"What was that for?" he asks, his eyes squinting in confusion again.

"Nothing, I'm just happy."

"You're happy?"

"Yeah, I am."

"And you're sure thats all it is? You sure you're not on something?

"Haha nope, and if I was I wouldn't be sharing it with you. Stud."

He punches me in the arm and the awkwardness that was present a few minutes ago is beginning to dissipate, as we continue to laugh and chat just like we used to.

It feels just like old times.

Almost.

CHAPTER FOURTEEN

Proper Stuff

It's after school. After detention. Jack and I are heading home together again. We thought about taking the bus but Jimmy Browne and Jenny Crawley were hanging around by the bus stop, harassing people as they passed, so we chose to walk home instead. Through the distillery. It's kind of weird but the distillery is starting to become our place. It's where everything seems to be happening between me and Jack.

"I don't know," Jack is saying. "I mean college is really expensive, especially if you can't get a grant and I'm not even sure what I'd want to do. There are so many options. Science, Arts, Business, so many courses to choose from. And did you hear what that guy said this morning. About how many people drop out after just the first term. I mean I wouldn't drop out I don't think, not after committing to going but who knows what could happen. You know what I mean?"

"Uh-huh."

"Are you even listening to anything I'm saying?"

"Uh-huh."

"Really?"

"Of course I am, college, so many options blah blah blah."

"Fine, what would you like to talk about then, seeing as I'm boring you so much," he says, turning away from me and scuffing the ground with the tips of his shoes.

"*You're* not boring me, what you're *talking about* is boring me. We get enough of that crap when we're actually at school. I'd rather not hear it outside school aswell. Plus I want to talk about you."

"Me?"

"Yes, you," I say, as he stares at me again, a sheepish look now etched onto his face. "Jack Hawkins. Tell me about yourself. Proper stuff. Not college choices and shit like that. I mean proper stuff."

"Proper stuff?"

"Yeah proper stuff. Like, who is Jack Hawkins really? What are your deepest darkest secrets? What turns you on?"

I send him a wink but he scowls back at me so I turn my attention to the abandoned building towering above us. I wait for him to speak but he has lapsed into silence, his lips pursed together tightly. Fucking hell, this kid. He is so closed off. So reluctant to share anything even remotely personal. What the hell can I do to get him to open up?

I look back to the building in front of me, a plan beginning to formulate in my mind.

"Fine then," I say breaking the silence. If you don't want to talk about yourself then let's have some fun."

He raises his eyebrows at me and I can see his eyes starting to twinkle. "What here?"

"No not that, you perv," I say, smiling. "Let's explore

this place. This place has been here for, like, forever and not once have I been inside it. Let's break in."

"What? No." The sparkle that was in his eyes a moment ago disappears. "We can't break in. We, er, we could get in serious trouble."

"Come on, don't be such a wuss. It'll be fun."

"I don't know, what if someone sees us and calls the police?"

"Does it look like anyone is around?" I ask, gesturing to the empty grounds and beyond, where all is quiet.

"No."

"Exactly. So come on."

I grab him by the elbow and pull him over to where the main doors to the factory are boarded up. The two large panels of wood covering the doors are weatherbeaten, broken and beginning to chip away at the sides, but still covering the doors, blocking our entry into the abandoned building. Every square inch of the wood is covered in graffiti. I spot several 'tags', including the one I left when I was twelve and came here with Dave and we felt like it was customary to leave our marks amongst the many others. It is smaller than the rest though, scribbled neatly and hidden amongst a load of others. Dave's is next to it, roughly the same size as mine.

I sling my bag off my shoulder, rifle through it, take out a marker pen and make my mark again, larger this time, ensuring that it covers over many of the ones that are long faded. I finish up and take a step back to admire my shoddy artistry. I hold the marker pen out for Jack to take but he just smiles and shakes his head.

"Come on, take it. Write something," I urge him.

"Nah, I'm alright."

"Do it, come on."

"No, I don't want to."

"Okay," I say, pocketing the marker pen and grabbing hold of one of the sides of the wood where it has already started to come away from concrete it was nailed to. "Help me with this."

Jack looks around and as if resigning himself to defeat, reluctantly slides his fingers in under mine, gripping the wood. We start to wiggle it a little. It comes away from the wall easier than I thought it would, the rusty nails slowly sliding out of the concrete. Probably a result of it being here for so long, water seeping into where the nails were hammered into the walls when it rains, freezing during the winter and slowly making the holes bigger so that the nails are no longer held tight by the concrete.

"Just a little bit more," I say, as we give it one last tug and it finally comes loose. We move it to the side and place it in front of the other large panel of wood, exposing half of the double doors of the distillery to the first ray of sunlight that it has seen in a long, long time.

I stop and think for a second. This is pretty fucking momentous. I mean this place has been boarded up for years and now here we are about to enter it. It must be what that Howard Carter guy felt like. You know the one who discovered Tutankhamun's tomb. I just hope we haven't released some evil curse like he did. I would like to still be alive in a week's time and I'm pretty sure Jack would too. But fuck it, curse or no curse, we need to go in. It is all part of my hastily thought out and still formulating plan to get Jack to open up to me. That is if it goes well, obviously. If it doesn't, it might just make him recede even more into himself. But if tread carefully, then hopefully that won't happen and I will finally know who the real Jack Hawkins is before we leave this distillery.

"Are you just gonna stand there staring at it all day?"

"Huh what?"

Jack is looking at me, his eyebrows meeting in the centre of his face. I must have zoned out again. I really need to get some control over that. It is happening way too often these days.

"You haven't said anything for ages, you've just been staring at the door."

"Oh, er, sorry. I was thinking."

"About what?" he says, regarding me suspiciously.

"Nothing important."

I reach my hand up and press hard against the door which resists, just as would be expected. I push it harder and the bottom start to give way but the centre, where the lock obviously is, holds firm. I lean against it with my shoulder, using the weight of my body to try and force it open but it still doesn't budge completely, the bottom still just the only part showing any sign of weakness. It would have to be so bloody hard wouldn't it, scuppering my plans. But if we can just get the bottom bit open, or even just a hole big enough, we might be able to crawl in.

"Here," I say to Jack, taking off my jumper and handing it to him. Wait here. I'll be back in two minutes."

"Why, where are you going?" he asks.

"You'll see."

Turning quicky, I break into a jog, heading towards the back of the old distillery grounds.

CHAPTER FIFTEEN

Exploration

I roll up my sleeves, the left first then the right, as I jog towards my destination: a large industrial sized skip filled with the rubble of a small building that stood just inside the grounds of the distillery, up until about two years ago when they (they being the local council) decided to knock it down for reasons only God knows. And for other reasons only God knows they decided to leave the skip here instead of taking it away.

I fling the metal doors wide open, which clang loudly, the noise reverberating through the grounds. I reach in, being careful not to scrape my arms too much and feel around, passing over several large pieces of rubble until I find one that can be lifted out with just one hand. I pull it out and examine it. Perfect. Small enough to fit in one hand, sharp enough on one side to hopefully pierce the doors. Holding onto it tightly I jog back to where Jack is standing, my jumper now folded neatly over his arm.

"Of course," he says, shaking his head but smiling slightly, clearly copping on to what my plan is.

I get down onto my knees and start hacking away at the bottom of the door. The wood of the door is in a much better condition than that external wood that was covering it and is harder to cause damage to than I expected. But after a few strikes some bits of wood begin to flake away. It takes a while to chop away the outline of a gap big enough for us to squeeze through, Jack watching me with apprehension.

I give one final hit with the stone and stand up. One hard kick should do it. So I stand with my back to the door, my palms and ass resting against it and raise my foot in front of me as Jack watches, clearly apprehensive. I bring my foot down, hard and fast, and it sends the piece of wood flying inwards, creating a jagged opening.

"Am I just amazing or what," I say, winking at Jack and raising my arms in a mock celebration.

"Meh, you're alright," he says, making it obvious that feats of strength are not qualities he's attracted to.

"Okay then, let's go."

I get to my knees and crawl in through the gap, pushing the piece of wood just broken off the door to the side, so that we dont get any splinters from it. I stand up and move out of the way, waiting for Jack to follow me. When he doesn't I crouch down and look through the gap at him. He looks nervous, his face beginning to pale. He must be scared that if we get caught it will affect his future prospects.

"I don't know about this Dean."

"What? Come on, it'll be fun. Just do this for me and we can do what you want to do after."

Scrunching his face up and bowing his head, he gets to his knees and crawls forward. I offer my hand to help him up when he gets through and he accepts it. When he is on his feet, brushing dust from the knees of his trousers, I turn around and take in everything. The place is huge. Cavernous. Looks way bigger on the inside than it does from the outside. Definitely some TARDIS shit going on here.

But the size of the place is not what is most impressive about it. The most impressive thing is the two lines of what I can only describe as giant, golden coloured, cylindrical containers with large pipes coming from the top of them running parallel to each other for the entire length of the building. These are obviously what were used to distill the alcohol when this place was in its prime. I notice one of the containers towards the back of the room has a gaping hole in it, the edges of which are charred and ragged, like something exploded through it or something.

But apart from that damaged container there are no obvious reasons why this place even went out of business, no obvious signs of disrepair or abandonment. There are enough of those huge containers to produce hundreds, if not thousands of barrels a week, it looks like. I walk over to the first one on my right and tap on it with my knuckles. The noise echoes throughout the entire building, the ringing seeming to come from every corner, seeming to resonate in my eardrums.

"This is so cool," I say, runnning my hand over the surface of the container feeling the smoothness of it underneath my fingers. "Imagine what this place would have been like when it was up and running."

"Yeah it must have been pretty cool," Jack says.

But I'm not sure if he really means that because the look on his face is telling a completely different story. He looks quite uncomfortable, so I take a step towards him, putting my plan into motion. I grab his hand and pull him close, bringing my other hand up and running it through his hair. His hair feels just as I would expect it to. Soft and silky. It slides gracefully through my fingers. He brings his hands up and drapes them across my shoulders, locking them together behind my neck. He leans his head forward, his perfect eyes glistening in the light, the golden container behind us reflected in the dark of his pupils.

Closing my eyes I press my lips against his, gently. I wait for him to take control, to take it further and after a few seconds he slides his tongue into my mouth, gently caressing mine. They slide around each other, creating a perfect rhythm, like two dancers that have spent years perfecting a perfectly balanced routine.

It feels amazing and I'm sure we could stay like this for hours (or until we need to breathe again) but I want him to do more, to take some control. Which is what I view as the first step to him being able to open up to me. If he feels like the one in control, then hopefully he will feel like being able to tell me more.

Using my right hand I slide it down the side of his body feeling through his jumper the toned body that he hides exceptionally well and with my left I grab his arm and place it on my waist. Once again I wait for him to take it further and eventually he does, as he begins to rub my waist, softly at first. Then really surprising me, he takes complete control, removing his hand from my waist and bringing it down to rest on my crotch.

Well, shit. I was not expecting that at all. He grasps my cock firmly, feeling it through the fabric of my trousers and it starts to get hard, growing bigger with every firm rub he gives it. Then, pulling his lips away from mine he licks them very slowly, very seductively and gets to his knees. He undoes the button and flies of my trousers and starts to slide them down, ready to expose my erection.

But as much as this is getting me going, I can't do it.

It is too much. I wasn't expecting him to go that far. It's too quick. I'm not ready for that. Not yet. So I grab Jack's hands and stop him, my now rock hard penis just about to spring out past the waistband of my underwear.

"Wait," I say, taking a deep breath in as I feel it throb against the taut waistband. I grab his hands and pull Jack ack up into a standing position. I raise my trousers back up, do up the flies and fasten the button.

"What's wrong?" he asks, looking upset.

"No there's nothing wrong. It's just... I'm not ready to go that far yet."

"I think you should tell him that," he says, gesturing to the very noticeable bulge in the front of my trousers. He reaches his hand out, ready to start rubbing me again but I block it, taking his hand into mine instead, weaving my fingers in between his.

"Please, I'm just not ready to go that far yet. It's too soon."

He looks at me, clearly dubious. He looks like he is about to protest, but when he speaks his voice is full of understanding. "Okay, it's cool. But if it's okay with you can we leave here please? I really don't like being in here."

I want to explore more, maybe move ahead with more of my already failing plan but if he doesn't like it then there is no point staying. It obviously won't work here.

"Sure. Let's go."

We walk over to the gap in the door we came through, still holding each other's hands. I let go of his and slip out through the gap, waiting for him to emerge. It takes longer than I expect. What the hell is he doing? For someone who said he doesn't like it he is taking his time leaving! When he does come his eyes are watery, his face looking a little...I want to say pained...

"Are you okay?" I ask. "You look like you're about to cry. I didn't mean to upset you. It's just I'm not ready to go that far yet."

"No, no, of course not, it's not that. I just didn't like being inside there. It creeped me out."

"But its just an old distillery," I say.

"I know. It's just....." He trails off into silence, looking down at the ground.

I don't understand. It wasn't creepy at all. It was actually pretty cool inside. One of the most impressive things I have ever seen in this shitty town. Not that we saw much of it, getting no more than ten feet inside it. But still, what we did see was great. But something about it has clearly spooked him. But I can tell he won't want to talk about it, so I'm not going to push it any further.

"Here, help me with this." I point towards the large panel of wood that we removed a little while ago. "We should probably try and put this back. Well, as best as we can anyway."

We each grab a side and slot it back into place, beside the other panel, pushing the nails back into the holes we ripped them from earlier. It slides in easily and wobbles a bit when we let it go but it settles when we step back. The holes are clearly knackered now, but it should stay in place as long as no one else goes near it.

"I should probably head home," Jack says.

"Okay cool," I say, picking my bag up from the ground where I left it. He has already started to walk away so I shout after him. "But text me, yeah?"

He raises his hand a little but doesn't turn around. I just hear his voice carrying back to me on the wind, it almost sounding like he is choking back tears.

"I will."

CHAPTER SIXTEEN

The Bigot

Saturday morning. Could actually be afternoon. I'm not sure. I am lying in bed, having just woken up. The drapes are still pulled, my room in almost total darkness, light just about creeping in through the gap at the side where it doesn't fully lie flush against the wall. I waited all last night for Jack to text me, even declining an offer from Dave and Luke to go to the cinema. But he never did. And I didn't text him either. I don't know why really, it just didn't feel like I should, the way he just walked off and all that after our exploration yesterday.

But you know, Jack is such a weird guy. One minute he is completely shy and reserved and the next he seems really confident and full of gusto. Like when he was tring to rip my trousers off yesterday. He was eager to get his hands (and probably more) on me. But then, afterwards, saying that the distillery really creeped him out, when it is one of the coolest places I've ever been in. I just cannot work the guy out. I cannot read him at all. It is so fucking frustrating. But I suppose I will just have to keep trying to get him to open up to me. I mean, who wouldn't want to open up to me eh? I'm amazing! (Yeah right!)

I kick the duvet off me and it lands in a heap on the

floor. I swing my legs over the side of the bed where they touch the floor. Wiggling my toes, I stand up and stretch my arms up over my head, towards the ceiling, to loosen my body up, to shrug off the last vestiges of sleep. I prise the drapes apart slowly, expecting to be hit by a ray of sunshine, considering how nice the weather has been the past few days. Instead all that is visible through the window is a sky shrouded heavily with clouds. White, fluffy clouds though. Not the grey thundery, clouds of rain. But still, they block out any sunshine trying to come through. Typical though, isn't it? Been nice all week and I've been stuck in school and detention and now, when I have a proper bit of free time, the weather turns.

It doesn't really matter though. It is not like I was planning on spending much time outdoors anyway. I just would have liked to have the option available. But I will probably end up doing what I do most Saturdays. See, I usually spend Saturdays with my dad (and brother Darren when he isn't working) down the local 'boozer' (which is a pub if you didn't know) watching 'The Football'. And yeah it is just as horrible as it sounds. A bunch of grown men, drinking pints, wearing the shirts of their favourite football clubs, swearing loudly any time one of the players fucks up.

But you're probably wondering why do I do it if it sounds horrible? Two reasons really. Firstly, it's tradition, both in our home and throughout the town. Always has been. Ever since me and my brother were kids, shit probably even since our grandparents were kids. If you are not seen spending time down the pub on a Saturday watching the football you are seen as being odd, a weirdo, as the outcast of the town. And secondly, because it is the only time I get to spend with my dad really and it makes him happy to think we have a shared interest. So yeah, even though I don't really like it, I do it to make my dad happy. Sounds stupid and soppy, I know. But that's just the way it is. And, I mean, why shouldn't I be nice to my family?

I have a quick shower, get dressed and head downstairs. My mum and dad are already in the kitchen. Mum is sitting at the table, Dad standing by the door to the back garden, one hand in his pocket, the other holding a large mug in front of himself, about waist height. Neither of them look happy. Mum looks a little stressed and Dad looks really tired, his eyes puffy and eyelids heavy, like he hasn't slept in weeks. But, when they notice me, walking through the door into this what already feels like a really strange moment, they smile.

"Morning," I throw out, a little wary.

Maybe they have been fighting. Though usually when they are the whole street knows. And they wouldn't usually be together in the same room if they'd had an argument. So it has to be something else. Not a death in the family. They would have said already. Divorce? Possible, but not likely. Neither of them could afford the legal fees. One of them is sick? Again they would have said, they wouldn't keep something like that a secret. But there is something. I can sense it in the air. Maybe it would be better to steer clear of the kitchen...

"Afternoon you mean," Dad says pointing up at the clock on the wall. "It's almost one."

"Oh, I didn't realise. You should have called me," I say, reaching up to take the cereal out of the press. I grab a bowl from the press and pick up a spoon from the drainer and sit down at the table, opposite my mum.

"So what time are we heading down to Faughs at?" I

ask my dad. Faughs is the name of that local pub I mentioned earlier.

"Actually, I was thinking we'd stay here today," Dad says. Watch the match here, have a few beers."

"Oh, right. Okay," I say, taken aback. Now I know something is definitely wrong. Dad has never, ever not gone to the pub on a Saturday to watch the match. It is pure sacrilege in his eyes. "Is everything okay?"

"Yes of course," my dad says, although I can see in his tired eyes and the way he looks across at my mum, as if for some form of support, that that is clearly a lie. "Just fancied a change."

"Yeah," Mum says, nodding and smiling thinly. "It will be good to stay home for a change, relax and maybe save a bit of money." She lets out a soft giggle that doesn't match her expression, but my dad looks uncomfortable and lifts the mug up to his mouth, draining the last of whatever was in it.

"Okay cool", I say, beginning to shovel spoonfuls of cereal into my mouth, really wracking my brains to think what could be wrong that would make my dad diverge so much from the norm.

I spend the next hour just hanging out in the living room, flicking through TV channels, not settling on any one in particular. While some quaint bakery show plays in the background, I take my phone out of my pocket and start browsing through some of the apps. Facebook, Insta, all the usual ones. I don't feel like posting anything though. But there is something I want to do, that I've been thinking of doing since my dad said we were staying at home today. I go to the messaging app and start typing.

Hey whats up?

A nice casual start.

Staying at home to watch the match. Wanna come over? It'll just me me and my dad, maybe Darren if he gets off work early.

I read over it and hit send.

I wait a few minutes for a reply which comes in with a buzz, my phone vibrating softly in my hand. It is short. To the point.

Sure, I'm on the way.

My dad comes in to the living room and sits in his armchair facing the TV. His eyes are still heavy and tired looking. He sits slumped in the chair, almost becoming lost in the cushions and I notice some stubble growing on his chin, which isn't like him at all. He is usually clean shaven. Says he has to be for work. I have never seen him with any sort of facial hair, except, of course, in photographs of when he was a teenager. Large, furry moustaches must have been all the rage back in the eighties.

"Here," I say, tossing him the remote control for the TV. "The match will be starting soon."

He catches it and immediately changes from whatever channel it was on to the one showing the match where the pre match talks are on. A group of men in pristine, slim fitting suits sit around a table discussing proposed strategies and predicting potential outcomes. Why they have to do so much analysis baffles me. Why can't they just watch the match, let it all unfold before them?

"Dean, go get me a beer will you," my dad says, the tone of his voice suggesting that it's more of an order than a request.

"Er, yeah sure."

I leave my spot on the sofa and head into the kitchen. My mum is sitting at the table flicking through a magazine. She looks up, smiling. "Everything okay son?"

"Yeah, fine. Dad wants a beer," I say pulling open the fridge door.

I see my mum, in my peripheral vison, close her eyes and notice how her chest rises as if she is suppressing a sigh, her smile gone. I reach in and bundle a few of the cold beers into my arms. It will save me any further trips if he wants more. I turn away from the fridge, using my foot to swing it shut. The beer bottes rattle in my arms as glass knocks against glass. I stop in the doorway and half turn back to face my mum who has resumed flicking through her magazine.

"Mum."

"Yeah son?."

"Is everything okay with Dad? He seems... I dunno... a bit off or something."

She does't look up from her magazine but she closes her eyes again and her lips move silently for a moment.

"Everything is fine love, he's just under a lot of pressure at work. He's dealing with some very difficult clients at the moment."

"And that's all it is?"

"Of course, it's nothing to worry about at all. He'll be glad to see the back of them."

I can tell she is lying. That it is definitely not just regular work pressures. He has been dealing with work pressures for years. But if they are determined to keep it a secret then I'm not going to push it, not going to probe into their business. And I suppose if it was really bad they would have said something.

"Okay, cool, just wanted to check," I say, shrugging and head back into the sitting room.

My dad frowns at the amount of bottles in my arms

but doesn't say anything, just reaches out and grabs one from the top of the bundle. He twists the cap off and takes a long swig from the bottle, the beer foaming up the neck and spilling a little down the sides of it when he releases it from the suction of his lips. I dump the rest of the bottles onto the other armchair, within my dad's reach. The doorbell rings just as I'm about to sit down and my dad lets out a loud tutting sound.

"What's the point of that idiot having a key if he doesn't use the damn thing" he says, a sort of bitternes evident in his tone.

"It's not Darren, Dad, it's Dave. I texted him to come over seeing as we were staying here today."

"Oh, right." He takes another long swig from the bottle in his hand, almost emptying it and I go out into the hall, opening the door for my friend.

"Hey."

He steps into the hallway, takes off his coat and hangs it on the end of the bannister, like he does every time he comes over.

"What's up Turner? Started yet?"

"Nah not yet, just about to."

I close the door and we head into the living room. My dad has already started on his second bottle of beer, the first bottle now empty, discarded on the floor beside him. Dave looks at the pile on the other chair. Fuck! It may have been a huge mistake, bringing that much alcohol to a man who is clearly going through some shit.

"Hey, Mr. Turner, how's things?" Dave asks, as he takes a seat on the sofa, stretching his legs out and putting his arms up behind his head, his muscles bulging.

My dad just makes a gruff, 'mhm' sound in response. Dave looks at me and I shake my head to indicate that he shouldn't worry about it as I sit down beside him . On the TV the pre match talks have ceased and the camera pans across the football field where the players of each team are lined up facing each other, two opposing sides about to go to battle. The camera then zooms in on the referee, a tall, blacked haired man, with a hairstyle that is about thirty years out of date, who tosses a coin to decide which side gets to kick off. Then he places the ball in the centre of the pitch, blows his whistle and off it goes.

The ball travels up and down, up and down, each team failing to score a goal. Each time it gets close to the net of the team in blue my dad leans forward in his chair a little and proceeds to swear louder each time they miss. He is also getting louder with each beer he drinks. Like each one is applying pressure to the 'increase volume' button. The referee on the screen blows his whistle, indicating half time, when each side of the battle gets a few minutes break, to assess the damage done, to reassess their strategies.

My dad makes a noise that sounds like a growl, yes an actual growl, as he drops yet another empty bottle onto the floor beside him. He looks really dishevelled now, his shirt all hitched up under his chin, his face in a scowl, not like himself at all. I glance sideways at Dave, wishing now that I hadn't invited him over.

"Not a great game is it Mr. Turner," Dave says to my dad, edging forward on his seat.

"Fucking shit game. Not a fucking clue any of them. The whole sport is gone to shit if you ask me. But it's bound to happen when they're letting the likes of him play."

My dad waves his arm at the screen of the TV where it is replaying a near miss by a young player who I recognise immediately. I only recognise him because he was all anyone down the pub could talk about last Saturday. See, he is the first publicly gay footballer, having just come out in the press a couple of weeks ago. So when he was playing last week there was a lot of debate among all the 'men' as to whether he should be playing at all now that everyone knows he is gay. Most agreed that it didn't matter what side he liked his bread buttered on as long as he could play well. But there were a few who were so vehemently against the idea of a gay man playing football that several fist fights almost broke out.

Through it all though my dad didn't say much, only just nodding or shaking his head, depending on what was said, the nodding generally in support of anyone who said the young guy shouldn't be allowed to play anymore. And I don't like what he said, just now, about "letting the likes of him play." No I do not like that at all. It really shouldn't matter what someone's sexual preference is. It really shouldn't matter at all. And I know I probably shouldn't say anything. Not when he is drunk like this. But I have to. I can't just sit by and let him go around insinuating stupid things like that. I have to say something. I would be just as bad as all of those bigoted fools down the pub if I keep quiet. I turn away from the TV and look at him.

"What do you mean by that Dad?"

"What?

"What you said just now about 'letting the likes of him play'," I wave my hand, like my dad did, at the TV screen where the young footballer's near miss is being replayed for a second time. "You can't say things like that."

"Can't say things like that," he says, mimicking me, like a child would. "Shut up, Dean. I'll say whatever I Goddamn please."

"What the hell Dad? I think you need to stop drinking."

"Don't you dare tell me what I need to do. And I'll say whatever I Goddamn please in my own house and you won't tell me any different." He moves forward in his chair and glares at me. "It's poofs like him that are ruining the game."

I start to say something back but close my mouth, not really sure what to say. I just can't believe my dad is being like this. I've never seen my dad act this aggressively before in my life. It is actually pretty frightening, him glaring at me the way he is and getting angry. I should probably go and get my mum, see if she can calm him down. But what if he just starts going mad at her. Then shit would really hit the fan. And Dave would witness it and that would not be good for him. He comes here to escape that sort of shit from his own house, not to suffer more of it.

I must have zoned out again because I am suddenly aware that my dad is standing over me, his finger poking me hard in the chest. I can smell the bottles of beer he drank earlier strong on his breath.

"And who do you think you are talking to me like that and then not listening, eh? Ungrateful little shit."

I stand up quickly and he staggers backwards, almost losing his balance and falling over. But he steadies himself using the arm of the chair. He starts to move towards me, his hand balling into a fist at his side but I duck out of the way.

"Just fuck off then. Little ungrateful bastard," he says, flopping himself down into his seat in front of the TV. He starts to say something else but I don't wait around to listen, darting out into the hallway, although I can hear him mumbling to himself as I take the stairs two at a time. I slam the door of my room behind me. and sit down on my bed, anger starting to bubble up in me, my chest heaving heavily.

Seriously, what the fuck was that all about? I have never seen my dad have an outburst like that before. I've never seen him down drinks like that either. Something is seriously up with him. But that's no excuse and, you know what, at least I am aware of his views now. His archaic, moronic views. Calling people 'poofs'. And insinuating, not very subtly that people like that innocent footballer shouldn't be playing the game just because of his sexual orientation. What a load of bullshit. Bullshit!

He is clearly a homophobe. Maybe that is something I should have clocked on to a long time ago. And now, thinking back, I think I did to be honest. A few sly remarks here and there over the years, agreeing with those pricks in the pub. But I just brushed it aside, had no reason to pay any heed to it. But now I have. And I feel somewhat ashamed. And confused. And all mixed up. And mad as hell. I raise my hands up to my head and rub my temples, a headache starting to form.

There is a gentle tap on the door and I look up to see Dave stick his head around. Shit! I forgot I left him alone with my dad downstairs, when I came storming out of the living room. Must have been awkward.

"Safe to come in?"

"Yeah of course." He slips the rest of himself into the room and closes the door behind him and I move up on the bed, giving him space to sit down.

"That was-", he hesitates.

"Fucked up," I finish for him.

"Well I was gonna say intense but yeah, what the hell was that all about Turner."

"I really just haven't a fucking clue man."

"I've never seen your dad like that."

"Nope, me either."

"But you aswell Dean, man, it's like you were just completely gone. Your eyes were sort of glazed over. That's why your dad got up and started poking you in the chest. It's like you weren't even listening."

Fuck! Dave just called me Dean. He only calls me Dean when he's worried. Or afraid. Or both. Have I really been zoning out that much? I mean, I have always been one to zone out, go into my own mind a little bit, but is it really becoming that much of a problem, that my eyes are glazing over? I need to get a handle on that, before something bad happens.

"Shit. I dunno man. I didn't even realise," I say. "Sorry you had to be there for that."

"Don't worry about it, I've dealt with worse, as you know."

That is true. I know about everything that Dave has had to deal with at home, so I know that he would be the perfect person to get advice from. But I really don't wanna talk about it, any of it right now, I need to just clear my head of everything.

Bad idea? To bottle everything up? Probably. But I just don't want to talk yet. If I start talking I might reveal too much, about me, about Jack. About everything that we have been doing. So I can't say anything.

Instead I stand up and turn my small TV on, then the games console, waiting for the little green circle to illuminate. I toss one of the controllers to Dave and we start to play.

We chat, eat and play for ages, hours, until the room is dark and the only source of light in he room is the TV, where Dave's character has just died a grisly death and my character is left on the battlefield alone. He stands up and puts the controller on the desk, next to the empty pizza boxes that contain nothing of the pizzas we ordered earlier.

"I should probably head home."

"Yeah cool, this was a laugh, considering everything that happened this week."

"Ha yeah, pretty crazy week alright." He puts his hand on the door handle but stays facing me. "But er, you gonna be okay here, you know after..."

He looks me dead in the eye and even though he is half in darkness I can still see enough of his face to make out a look of true concern for me.

"Yeah, of course I will, he's just going through some shit that he hasn't said anything about. But it will be fine. Thanks."

"Not a problem, Turner, you know where I am if you need me. See you later."

"Yeah, talk later, Stud."

He opens the door and heads out onto the landing. I lay back on my bed in the semi darkness, listening as his footsteps descend gently down the stairs and he exits through the front door, stepping out into the night.

CHAPTER SEVENTEEN

Game On!

I did not sleep well last night. At all. Probably only drifted off for a couple of hours. Tossing and turning all night. Completely restless, everything from the past week playing over and over in my mind. The good and the bad. I even woke up drenched in sweat at one point. That's why I'm laying on my bed naked, the sweat soaked clothes in a bundle on the floor. I look over at my desk, the two controllers still sitting on top since last night. I slide my hand under my pillow, pick up my phone and power it on. It vibrates in my hand a few times, buzz after buzz, as notifications pop up one after another on the screen. I swipe them all off, not interested in seeing updates from Facebook right now.

I toss it on to the bed beside me but it vibrates again. I pick it up, expecting to see just another Facebook update, that I will inevitably just swipe off the screen, but my stomach does a little flip when I Jack's name flash across the screen.

Hi Dean. Sorry I didnt text sooner- wasnt feeling great. Listen, I just found out my mum won't be here today so Im gonna be here all by myself. Wanna come over? I understand if you dont if it feels like rushing things but I am just gonna be here. By myself. All day. Alone. Anyway let me know as soon as you see this.

I start typing.

Yeah, definitely I'll be the-

I stop, my thumbs hovering above the onscreen keyboard. I press the back space key until all the words have disappeared. I just need to think for a second. Is this really what I want? I mean, after everything that happened with my dad yesterday, is this really the best course of action? He is clearly opposed to men being gay. So what would he say if he found out I was, well not gay exactly, but have been kissing a guy, Jack, who is very clearly gay. And if I go to his house and we start doing stuff and he finds out about that. Will he have another outburst like he did yesterday. Worse maybe? Would he do more than just poke me in the chest?

Maybe I just won't text back. Ignore it. I mean he didn't text me after we had been at the distillery again on Friday. After he was about to rip my trousers off.

No, you know what. I ball my hand into a fist and drop it down onto the matress, the noise of the springs being compressed reverberating through the silence of my room. Fuck it. I'm going. I don't give a shit. My dad won't know, he won't find out. I'll make sure. Anyway, he said his mum won't be home. And that he will be alone. So I'm going. We will be alone, so I don't need to worry about getting caught. I start quickly typing again, my thumbs working frantically. I read over my message confirming I will be over this afternoon and hit send. No going back now.

I stand up and look down at my body. I suck in my

belly a bit even though there is no need, I am as slim as I always have been. Not as toned as Jack, not by a long shot. There is definitely no six pack on Dean Turner. But I'm not completely out of shape either. I wriggle my toes on the floor and move my hips from side to side. Hmm. Things are starting to get a bit bushy. I should probably do someting about that.

I open the lowest drawer on my desk and rummage around until I find what I'm looking for. The three attachments, of different cutting lengths, for my electric shaver in the bathroom. It's been a while since anyone has seen me naked. I have some grooming to do.

I turn the corner and walk up the street that Jack's house is on. Number Twenty Seven. I remember from the other day. I keep walking until I reach it, put my hand out and start to push the gate open but stop halfway, hit by a sudden wave of panic. Shit. Should I have brought something? Like some beer or some chocolate or something? Does Jack even drink beer? Or eat chocolate? He probably doesn't, considering how fit he is. But, fuck, I should have brought something, shouldn't I? Or would that be too... date-like? Is that even what this is? I really have no fucking idea what I'm doing do I? Maybe I should just turn around. Go back home. Forget about this. I look up at the house. The drapes in the downstairs window twitch a little, so if someone inside has seen me, I can't just slip away now...

So I take a deep breath and walk up the concrete driveway, my breathing becoming more laboured, each intake coming faster and ever shallower. I reach out, about to lift the outside flap of the letterbox but the door swings open in front of me. My breath stops completely. He is standing there in a pair of shorts, similar to the ones he wore the other day when I came. But that's all he is wearing. Well those and a pair of grey sliders, you know the ones with a flat sole and just a single strap of material that goes over the top of your foot. I am pretty sure my mouth is hanging open forming an O shape and if I don't close it or speak soon I will probably start drooling. So I opt for a simple greeting.

"Hey."

"Hi."

"Thanks for inviting me over."

He smiles, his lips curling up at the sides of his mouth. "You usually say that when you're leaving somewhere, not when you haven't even been in yet. So come in. And er, close your mouth, your'e gonna catch flies if you leave it hanging open like that."

He steps out of the way and I walk in past him, stopping just a few feet into the hallway, not really sure what to do. Do I keep walking into the living room, where I've been to before or do I wait for Jack to direct me where to go? I hover, waiting. Jesus when did I become such a nervous person?

But I don't have to wait long because Jack closes the door, brushes past me and heads into the living room. I follow after him, looking down at his calves as he walks, the muscles tightening and relaxing as he moves forward with each step. The TV is on, a 'Game Paused' logo filling the screen, which I immediately recognise as being from the game Dave and I were playing last night.

I gesture towards the screen. "What level are you on?"

"You play this?"

"Of course I play this, who doesn't play this!."

"Well, look who has good taste. But we already knew that or else you wouldn't be so obsessed with me."

"Obsessed? I'm not obsessed, I'm...", I can feel my cheeks starting to turn turn red, the sweat practically turning to steam as soon as it seeps out and touches my skin.

"Relax I'm just kidding. I'm on level twelve', he says picking up a pair of controllers and throwing one to me. "You?"

"Shit I'm only on level nine. And I was playing for hours yesterday. You must be pretty good."

"I'm alright I guess. Let's see how good you are."

He presses a series of buttons on his controller and the screen goes live. The controller in my hand vibrates and the screen splits in two, Jack's character occupying the top half of the screen, while my newly introduced character, with a full bar of health, takes up the bottom half.

Game on!

CHAPTER EIGHTEEN

Tell Me Everything

I am sitting on Jack's couch, a little awkwardly to be completely honest. We stopped playing the game a few minutes ago. He is gone into the kitchen, getting us some drinks. I look around the living room, comparing it again to the outside of the house. Inside is so pristine, so neat and tidy, while outside is shabby and honestly just decrepit looking. It's strange. There must be a reason for it though. I'll have to try and bring it up with Jack later if I think of it.

He walks back in, two pint glasses of what looks like beer in his hands. He gives one to me and sips from his own one. I take a long swig from mine, confirming that it is in fact beer. And not a bad tasting beer either.

"I can see how you were on level twelve, while I'm lagging behind on level nine. You annihilated half the enemy's squad in one run. That's impressive."

"Well thanks. Guess I just had a lot of practice playing video games when I was younger. I used to play them a lot with my dad."

"I see. He wasn't here when I was here last time

and when you texted you just mentioned your mum. Is he...?", I don't know how to finish the question. It is the first time Jack has mentioned his dad and I can sort of see that strange look beginning to distort his face again. Maybe something happened. He ran off? His parents divorced and not happily?

"He's not here. Hasn't been for a while."

"Oh right, okay."

I don't say any more. Jack takes another sip from his glass and I take another large swig from mine. He stands up, glass in hand and starts to walk out past me.

"Come on, let's go upstiars."

I follow close at his heels, our footsteps falling into sync as we ascend. The layout of the house is similar to my own. Three bedrooms, each with a door branching off the landing, a small airing cupboard nestled between the second and third bedroom, the bathroom at the far end. Jack leads me to the bedroom I suspected would be his, the second biggest, after the master.

He opens the door, swinging it wide and I am hit by a pure wave of purple. Almost everything in the room that you can lay your eyes upon, apart from the floor and a desk that is a deep black, is purple. The drapes- purple. The bedclothes- purple. Even the lampshades, of the big main light and the smaller lamp on top of his desk, are a light purple colour. It is a bit overwhelming and just a complete and utter contrast to my modest cream and pine coloured bedroom at home.

He sits down on the bed and I stay standing by the desk, still just taking everything in, the sheer purple-ness of it all. How bold it is. How out of character it is. Or seems. Or does it, actually? I mean how much do I really know about Jack. Not really a whole lot, now that I think about it. But I guess now is my chance to get to know him better. I mean he did invite me over after all. He obviously wants me to know more about him now.

"Jesus, you must really like purple?"

"What? No, I hate purple."

"You hate pur...then why is everything...."

"I'm kidding, of course I like purple, do you really think I'd have this much of it if I didn't like it?"

"Well, no, obviously not", I reply, smiling a little and shaking my head. "You know you are just the hardest person to read. I just cannot figure you out at all." I move over and sit beside him on the bed, leaning back a little so I can look at him clearly.

He purses his lips and squints at me. "Is that a bad thing though? I mean isn't it better to be on guard than to let everyone know every intimate detail about yourself?"

"Well, yeah, I guess you need to be on guard to a certain extent, but I know practically nothing about you, Jack Hawkins." He scrunches his nose at my use of his full name.

"Well what do you want to know?" he asks, leaning back onto his pillow, his elbow creating a massive dent in the middle of it.

"Everything."

"Everything?"

"Yeah, like tell me everything there is know about Jack Hawkins."

"Okay, sure. Why not? My name is Jack. I'm sixteen years old. I have blue eyes and I clearly like the colour purple." He gestures at everything around the room as if I hadn't already noticed I was sitting in a sea of purple.

"Yeah, fool, that's the sort of stuff I know already. I

mean tell me some deeper stuff."

"Deeper stuff?"

"Yes, like stuff that matters. For instance I can tell you that I had a major fight with my dad yesterday for being a homophobic prick."

"Shit, really? Why?"

"Just over him insinuating that gay people shouldn't be allowed to play football. I didn't like that so I challenged him over it."

"Wow. Intense."

"Yeah, so tell me something about your life that matters. Like why are you so hot and cold all the time? Sometimes you come across really outgoing and confident, but most of the time, especially at school, you come across as really sy and timid. Why?"

He looks at me, his eyes searching mine, clearly having some kind of internal struggle. Maybe he doesn't think he can trust me. I reach my hand out and put it on his leg, feeling the soft hairs brush against my palm and fingertips. "You can trust me Jack."

"I know. There's just some stuff I'm not ready to talk about yet." He looks down at my hand resting on his leg and continues. "But okay, the reason I come across as such a loser at school is because those morons make life hell for me. People like Jimmy Browne and his gang of Neanderthals are just cruel. You know, people like him used to beat me up *every single day*." He puts an emphasis on the last three words and even though he is concentrating on the wardrobe several feet away from him, not looking at me, I can see the pain etched across his face. He must have been through hell. "I never have a break from it. Even people who are normally pretty nice can be so evil sometimes, like your friend Dave. So I just decided a long time ago to keep to myself, to try and stay off their radar, not that it ever works much either way. They can never just leave me be."

I don't know how to respond, so I just rub his leg gently and hope my face looks as empathetic as I feel right now. I can actually feel my heart constricting, as if trying to absorb just a fraction of the suffering that he seems to have been through.

"I'm sorry Jack, that you have to put up with all that bullshit. And I'm sorry for people like Dave. I promise he won't ever be like that again. I'll make sure of it."

"You don't need to apologise and you don't need to do that. It's not your responsibility to manage how people behave. You are one of the few good ones. I guess that's why I seem so confident around you. Because I feel like I can be. I feel like I can be myself."

"You can be," I say, my hand still caressing his leg.

His skin underneath the curly black hairs feels so soft, yet the strong muscle is evident. I take my hand from his leg and he looks over into my face. I pull my entire body up onto the bed, get into a crawling position and move towards him. I stop when my face is just millimetres away from his, and using my left hand, reach up and put it on his cheek. His skin is warm. I put my lips on his and let him kiss me. I feel his tongue slide into my mouth, massaging mine forcefully, but also with care.

I feel his hand make its way around my body, on my shoulder, my back, my hip, everywhere. He grabs the bottom of my t-shirt with both hands, pulling it up over my head, our lips breaking apart momentarily while he throws it on the floor, before being sucked back together like two strong magnets.

My hands explore more, feeling around his body, the

muscles hard and lean under my fingertips. I move my body in closer to his, feeling him growing though the thin material of his shorts. I start to grind on him, my own cock pulsating with every gyration. He breaks away from me and pulls his shorts off, dumping them on the floor. I undo the buttons on my own trousers and remove them along with my boxers, throwing them aside where they land on top of Jacks shorts.

We are in front of each other on our knees, our cocks side by side, almost touching, his slightly longer than mine, by about an inch or so. But mine has more girth. We reach down and take them into each other's hands, each of us gripping hard and stroking. He pushes me down onto my back and with one hand cupping my balls, while the other gently scrapes at my stomach, he takes me into his mouth.

CHAPTER NINETEEN

Purple Shadows

It is starting to get dark outside, and even darker inside Jack's bedroom where we are laying together, his head on my chest. Jack sits up and gets out of the bed. I watch his ass cheeks wiggle as he walks over to switch on the lamp on his desk. He almost seems to glide back over and lays down beside me, our naked bodies touching, both of us now completely flaccid and exhausted.

I prop myself up on one of my elbows and put my other hand on his chest. I move it slowly down his body, tracing the outline of his six pack, running it over the small trail of hair that sits between his belly button and pubic area (which he has trimmed down to a stubble a similar length to my own) still fascinated by how fit his body is and how he hides it so well at school.

"Are you gonna tell me how the fuck you get to be so fit or is it another big Jack Hawkins secret?"

"No big secret really. I'm a champion swimmer. Or at least I was until a few months ago."

"Bullshit."

"Not bullshit. Look up on top of the wardrode."

I look up and notice a deluge of trophies that I didn't see until now. I guess I was so overwhelmed by all of the purple that they just didn't register with me. They all have either a small figure on top or a picture of a figure all in various swimming or diving poses. And there isn't just one or two trophies. There is a whole pile of them. This kid must be amazing. And now I guess there is finally an explanation to why he is so fit. Swimmers are incredible athletes.

"Well, fuck me."

"I thought I just did."

"Funny." I tilt my head to the side and roll my eyes which he smiles at. "I never would have guessed though. I mean that's pretty amazing. That's something you should tell people about."

"Yeah, maybe, but it's too late anyway. I don't swim anymore."

"Why not?"

"Oh nothing really I just had a bit of a health issue a few months ago and the doctor said I shouldn't swim for a while."

"Is it anything serious?"

I pull my hand away from his chest. He looks at me and starts laughing. He knows what I'm thinking.

"Don't worry, it's nothing you can catch. Just a heart thing. Wasn't getting enough oxygen apparently. But it's dealt with now. Nothing to worry about."

He grabs my hand and puts it back on his chest, his own hand resting on top of it. I look around the room at all of the purple again, noticing all of the different shadowy shapes being thrown up onto the walls by the light from the lamp and how they have all taken on a purple hue, due to the light purple coloured lampshade.

"That's pretty cool," I say, lifting my hand up into the air and twirl it around, watching as it casts a shadow onto the wall beside me.

"What is?"

"The way the shadows look because of all the purple. Purple shadows. Very cool."

"Oh yeah, that is cool. Completely unintentional too. But, yeah, now I have purple shadows."

I lay back down, my head resting close to Jack's. I think about what just happened between us, how good it felt kissing him, having him in my hand, being with him, being inside him, his legs resting on my shoulders as I thrust into him.

But there is something I need to ask him, something that I realise now has been at the back of my mind all week, something that I should have asked before becoming so intimate with him.

"Why did you do it?"

"Do what?"

"Kiss me."

"Because that's what you're supposed to do when you're having sex Dean. Oh my god was this your first time?" He turns onto his side and looks into my face.

I stare back at him, seeing the corners of his mouth itching to form a smile. He reaches up and pushes a strand of hair away from my forehead.

"Shut up. I mean the first time. At the distillery. After the detention. Why did you kiss me? You knew I had a girlfirend."

"Oh, well I knew you two were going to break up."

"What. How the hell could you have known that? Psychic as well as an Olympic athlete now are you?"

"No, I saw them."

"Saw who?"

"Dave and Karen."

"You saw Dave and Karen?"

"Yeah, I saw them, that morning. Together I mean. She was sitting on his lap and they were kissing. They stopped when they saw me and Dave threatened me, saying that if I told anyone he would kill me. I suppose that's why he attacked me at lunch the same day. Just to intimidate me, I guess, to make sure I kept to my word that I wouldn't say anything."

◆ ◆ ◆

I pull the gate closed behind me and start walking, a definite spring in my step. I have never done any drugs and I don't think I ever will but if they are capable of making you feel half as good as I feel right now then I can kind of see the appeal. I mean I have never felt so content, so... I dont know, what is the word... euphoric. Yeah... euphoric. I don't even care that Jack didn't say anything sooner about seeing Dave and Karen together. He was obviously intimidated by Dave. Plus it all turned out good anyway. I have just had the best sex I have ever had and I literally feel like I am walking on clouds, the concrete underneath me not concrete, but soft springy clouds. This is a feeling I never had when I was with Karen. At least not to this extent. Is this what love, real love, feels like? It must be.

I head straight into the kitchen after taking off my shoes and leaving them at the foot of the stairs when I enter my house. My mum is sitting at the kitchen table, her laptop (that she barely knows how to operate by the way) opened in front of her. She closes it down softly and smiles at me as I walk to the fridge, about to prise it open and see what is available to wolf down. I am starving.

"There are some leftovers in the microwave for you love. Just stick it on for a couple of minutes."

"Cool, thanks Mum."

I press the buttons on the microwave and watch as the inside of it lights up and the glass turntable and plate inside begin to rotate. I pull some cutlery from the drawer, fill a glass up with water from the tap and place them on the table opposite my mum.

"Good day?" my mum asks.

"Yeah pretty good."

"Where did you go?"

I think about lying and saying I was with Dave all day. My mum doesn't know Jack and she loves Dave so would be unlikely to question anything if I say I was with him. But what's the point. I will just tell her I was with Jack. I don't have to be specific. I don't have to give any of the details. Not that I would be cringey enough to tell my mum about my sex life.

"Just with a new mate."

"A new mate? Who?"

"Just a guy from school. You probably don't know him. Jack Hawkins. Lives around by Rykers Field."

"Hawkins....Hawkins....Not Louise Hawkins lad is it?"

"Oh, er, I dunno Mum, I didn't ask what his mum's name is. I'm not a creep."

"God, Dean, knowing people's names doesn't make you a creep."

The microwave pings and I take the dish out, a tea towel folded in half between my hands so I don't burn them. I put it on the table and start eating straight away, not giving it a chance to cool down.

"I know Mum, it's just a phrase, but yeah it probably is his mum. She's kinda short, young for a mum of someone my age."

"Sounds like her alright. I think her partner used to work with your dad in the distillery before it closed."

"Oh. I didn't know that."

That's funny. Jack didn't say his dad used to work at the distillery when we were there the other day. Maybe he doesn't know. He said his dad hasn't been around for a while. He probably took off after the distillery closed. I can tell him though. Can be something we have in common.

And maybe I should think about changing my room a little. I don't have to go to the extremes that Jack has gone to and go all out purple. Just something small. Break up all the cream and plain old blandness that occupies it currently. Get some purple shadows of my own.

"Mum," I say, still shovelling forkfuls of food into my mouth. "Any idea where I can get a purple lampshade?"

CHAPTER TWENTY

The 'Date'

Monday. It is after school but I'm still here. No surprise. It is the start of my second week of detention. I saw Jack this morning. I wanted to sit beside him too and had my bag off and was almost taking my place beside him when I heard Jimmy Browne's voice pipe up from behind me. I didn't catch the entirety of what he said but I definitely heard the words "faggot" "kill" and "after school". Then there was a round of raucous laughter from him and his gang as they kept staring at me. That made me panic a little and I quickly moved to my usual seat at the side of the classroom. I could tell Jack was feeling somewhat dejected and I feel terrible about it still. I really wanted to sit with him, but I have to do what I have to do to. To protect myself. But more importantly, to protect Jack.

Anyway that was this morning. Now I am standing outside the room scheduled for today's detention. It must have been a quiet day on the misbehaviour front because there doesn't seem to be anyone else coming along. Usually there would be a few more people milling around out here, waiting for the teacher to show up. And Jack should be here too, he still has to do the detentions, the same as me. But there is no sign of him yet.

I hear some footsteps coming from the other end of the corridor and look up to see Jack coming down the corridor, talking animatedly with Mr. Black, the P.E teacher. They both smile when they see me, although two very different types of smiles. One, a friendly 'how are you today smile', the other, one of lust. Mr. Black looks down at the roster and opens the door for us to enter.

"Only the two of ye today lads. If I had the final say I'd be letting ye go, but we have to stay unfortunately. The Boss Man says so. But don't worry, I've never had an ounce of trouble from either of ye so I won't make ye do any work or anything like that. Ye can just relax for a while. So, go on, in ye go."

He gestures for us to enter and I go in ahead of Jack. I head straight for the back of the room and beckon for Jack to follow me as I take a seat, throwing my bag onto the floor at my feet. Mr. Black settles in at the teachers desk, switching on the computer and beginning to scroll.

"This feels so weird." Jack's voice is soft, low, almost a whisper but not quite.

"What does?" I ask.

"Sitting here at the back of the room. I've never sat this far back before. The room looks completely different. Like I'm seeing everything from a completely different perspective."

"Yeah, I know what you mean. It just seems miles away from everything. Maybe that's why everyone sitting at the back of the room is so dumb," I say. "Maybe they can't actually hear or see anything."

"Ah, you've cracked it. Maybe we should publish a study on it. Become world famous scientists."

We laugh together and turn in our seats to face each

other more. Mr. Black is still focused on the computer screen in front of him. I stretch my leg out so that it is resting against Jack's. Even through the fabric of our school trousers I can feel the warmth emanating from him.

"Last night was amazing," I say.

"It really was."

"I'm not going to lie, it was the best sex I've ever had. Not that I'm saying I've had sex with a lot of people but it was definitely still the best."

"I can honestly say the same," Jack replies.

I notice a red tinge beginning to make its way up Jack's neck, into his cheeks. He opens his mouth as if he wants to say something further but closes it.

"What is it?" I ask. "You can say whatever you want. I think we're past not being ble to say stuff to each other."

"Yeah, totally, it's just I was wondering if, er, you want to maybe do something after detention instead of going straight home."

"Oh." I look at Jack, partly relieved. I thought he was going to say something about how I performed last night or something. I open my mouth to say yes I would love to, but an image of Jimmy Browne pops into my head quickly followed by one of my dad, so I just stare at him, thinking for a moment.

I would really love to but I cannot help but become a little panicked at the thought of Jimmy Browne or my dad or anyone at all really, seeing us out on a "date" together. It was one thing being alone together at Jack's house, but outside, in public... I mean how would they react? What would they say? I know my dad certainly wouldn't be happy and Jimmy Browne would probably call me a faggot and kick the living shit out of me. I don't know if I should. But then how would Jack feel if I said no? Ugh, I just don't know what to do.

I feel a knot forming in my stomach and Jack speaks again, the words only barely penetrating my thoughts.

"Dean? You okay? You haven't said anything for a few minutes."

"Oh, sorry, yeah. Look, Jack, I would love to but I'm not sure that I'm ready for like a "date" just yet." I do the cliche air quotes with my fingers as I say the word 'date'.

"Well it doesn't have to be a *date* as such. Like it can be just two friends hanging out. We don't ever have to call it a date."

"Okay... but still... what if someone sees us, like Jimmy Browne or someone from my fami-"

"Who cares really though? They don't know what's going on between us. We can just say that I'm helping you with school work." He raises his eyebrows at me but I just tap my hand on my knee, still really not sure.

"Okay, look," he continues. "If you are really worried about being seen by anyone then we can go to a place I know. It's miles away. No one from around here will be there."

I can see that he is really eager. The more I look at him, at his beautiful face, his wide, puppy dog eyes, his perfect lips just inviting me in, begging to be wrapped around my-

"Okay," I say, finally giving in. "Let's do it then. But it is one hundred per cent not a date."

◆ ◆ ◆

We step off the bus, the fresh air hitting us in the face, Jack leading the way. We were on the bus for ages. I don't recognise any of my surroundings. How does Jack even know his way around here?

"Where the hell are you bringing me, Jack Hawkins?"

"Don't worry we're almost there."

"Yeah but where is 'there' exactly? And how do you know where you're going? This is miles away from anything."

"You'll see when we get there and I'll explain how I know about it when we're eating."

"Eating?"

"Yeah, it's a restaurant."

"Jack, we said this wasn't a date. A restaurant feels like a date to me."

"Yeah but it's not a restaurant, restaurant. Not a fancy one. It's a fast food slash cafe type of restaurant thing. It's really cool. Anyway we're here now, so stop worrying."

Jack has stopped in his tracks and I almost bump into him. We are standing outside of a row of one storey buildings. I look up and see a glowing red neon sign above our heads that reads GINO'S CAFE. Jack walks forward and holds the door open for me. I walk in and he follows behind me. It is clear now what Jack meant when he said it was a fast food slash cafe type place. Immediately, when you walk in from the street, there is a standard takeaway counter where you just can just order your food, wait and then go. But over on the left, stretching back and seeming to wrap around, until I can't see any further, are lots of American, 'side of the motorway', diner style metal tables and chairs.

Jack leads the way again, and we settle at a table that has two menus, two glasses and a jug of water already set out. I pick up one of the menus but just hold it in my hands, not looking at it yet, just taking in everything around me. There aren't many people here, the two tables to our immediate left and right are empty. The place is clean, the walls or at least what I can see of them (because they are covered in various photographs, of people, of buildings- some black and white, some colour) are painted a kind of eggshell white colour. I don't know what it is about the place, but it has a very welcoming feel to it. I look across at Jack who is staring at me, all wide eyed.

"Well, what do you think of it?" he asks.

"Yeah, I think I like it."

"Good. I'm glad. This is my favourite place to eat. You won't need that by the way." He reaches over and takes the menu out of my hand, places it back to back with the other one and puts them flat down on the table to our right. "They do the best burger you will ever taste here, so don't even try and question it."

"Yes Sir," I say, laughing and giving a mock salute. "So how do you know about this place then? It's a bit out of the way isn't it."

"Yeah it is a bit." His face contorts the way it has done before. It is a look of real pain and sadness, distorting his features. "But, er, the swimming pool where most of my tournaments used to be held is a five minute walk away so I used to come here with my dad after every one, even if I lost, well especially if I lost, because he would want to cheer me up and we would always get the burger."

"Ah I see, that's pretty cool."

"Yeah..."

The look is still on his face. And I'm running out of patience now, I need to know why he gets like that some-times. Becuase I don't know if I've said something wrong or not. I just need to know.

"Jack?" He squints his eyes at me and places his hands together on the table, in front of him. "I notice sometimes that you get this look on your face when I say things sometimes, where your whole face just changes and drops and you just look... I don't know... sad. And I guess I just want to know if it's something I've said or done or...." I trail off into silence, just leaving the question hanging.

"No, it's nothing you've done, it's just... sometimes I get reminded of my dad and I guess my face just shows my emotions too much."

"Oh, right...," I pause for couple of seconds then continue. "You said yesterday that he hasn't been around for a while. Did he leave you and your mum or something?"

"No, he didn't leave us. He wouldn't have done that."

"Right, so what then, is he in prison or something?"

"No. He's dead."

"Oh. Shit. I had no idea. I'm really sorry."

Woah, the thought that Jack's dad would be dead didn't even enter my mind. I mean, you don't think like that, really. Especially with Jack being so young and Jack's mum is young for a mother of a sixteen year old, so I just assumed he would be young too. But maybe he wasn't. Or maybe he was and just had some illness or something. See, this is exactly why you shouldn't assume things and try to find things out before you are entitled to know. You end up sticking your foot in it.

"It"s cool," he says, looking at me with a reassuring smile. "How would you? I don't like speaking about it. I guess I never really got over it. But I guess maybe talking about it will help?"

"Yeah, it probably will."

I reach over and, being incredibly brave, take Jack's

hand into mine. I give it a squeeze and then thread my fingers through his. "You can talk to me about anything."

I see tears forming in the corner of his eyes but he blinks them back and smiles smiles at me. I smile back at him so he takes a deep breath and continues talking.

"He was my best friend, sad as that sounds. But like, as you know, I didn't have a good time in school, always getting beat up and retreating into myself and stuff. But my dad was always there for me. Always supportive. Always brought me to my swimming tournaments. Always cheered me on. Then one day while he was at work, at the old distillery, there was an accident, one of the containers exploded. He was closest to it and took the full force of it. That's why it closed down you know. They deemed it unsafe to work in after that. And I guess it just really fucked me up. I still can't even..."

I don't interrupt him, I just let him keep on talking, squeezing his hand every now and then, letting him know that I am listening, that I'm here. But shit, I never knew any of this. I didn't even know the reason for the distillery closing. That means my dad would have known Jack's dad. Would probably have worked closely with him. Fuck. If only I had known. I could have been a better friend to Jack over the years that we have been in school together. I could have, no, would have protected him.

CHAPTER TWENTY- ONE

Returning The Key

You know, I think I am falling in love with Jack Hawkins. Yes, I know that sounds stupid and cliche because I have only truly known the kid for a week and he has only just started opening up to me in these past twenty-four hours. But I have never felt this strongly about anyone in such a short period of time. My feelings for Karen were never this strong and the few times I had sex with her were nothing compared to how it was with Jack at the weekend. That was just leg shakingly mind-blowing.

Yesterday was pretty mind-blowing too, but for different reasons. I had no idea that Jack's dad was dead. Would never have guessed it either. I thought he was just someone who ran out out his wife and kid or something. Also, I really appreciate Jack opening up to me like that and telling me everything. It really does explain everything too. It's easy to understand now why Jack acts the way he does. Suffering how Jack has suffered would fuck anyone up. I am surprised he is still standing to be honest. There is no way I could handle something like that. Look how much I freaked out last week and that was nothing.

He really is a tough cookie, that kid.

Oh, wait, do you remember the key I 'borrowed' from Mr. Danvers? Yeah, I completely forgot I had that but this morning in Geography, when I reached into my bag looking for a ruler, to help draw a sketch map with, I pulled that out instead. I take it out of my shirt pocket and show it to Jack.

We are sitting at the back of today's detention classroom. Mr. Black is back in charge so he is letting us get on with our own thing again. There are a couple of other people here today though, so we don't have complete privacy but they are just some first year girls, so they take no notice of us. Jack doesn't look overly impressed with the story of how I managed to acquire the key.

"You're gonna say I should give it back aren't you" I say to him, twirling it between my fingers.

"Well, yeah, you shouldn't have even stolen it."

"I didn't steal it. I "borrowed" it." I do the cliche air quotes again with my fingers when I say the word borrowed. "I'm not gonna keep it indefinitely. I will give it back... eventually."

"Well, you shouldn't have "borrowed" it either, Dean. It's not really right. A student shouldn't have something like that. You should give it back."

"Jesus, okay Mr. Fun Sponge. We can bring it back to Mr. Danvers' office on the way home, okay?"

"Yeah, good. You know, responsibility is sexy."

I slip the key into my shirt pocket and turn away from Jack, crossing my arms over my chest. I am not a complete idiot. Obviously I would give the key back eventually but it would have been good to have a little bit of fun with it first. Like, we could have had access to anywhere in the entire school. Anywhere. We could have found out anything. But now I guess we will never even know what we could have known.

I hear a chair scraping on the floor and look up to see Mr. Black standing, arm raised in front of him, his eyes focused on the watch strapped to his wrist. He bobs his head up and down a little, mouthing silently, obviously counting down the seconds until it is time for us to go. I gather up my bag and sling it over my shoulder, ready to leave.

"Okay, time is up. Everybody out. Hurry up girls, we want to get out of here quickly."

I hurry out past him, sensing Jack following behind me and hear him say goodbye to the PE teacher as I walk on, heading straight for the principal's office. I make my way through the corridors, the eerie silence making me shudder. It is something I will never get used to. There is just something wrong about being able to hear your footsteps ring out and echo through the corridors. You really need that hustle and bustle of student activity for the place to feel right.

I reach the office and knock gently on the door, waiting for Mr. Danvers to tell me to come in. But there is no call to enter, just silence. I put my ear up to the door, listening for any sounds from inside. Nothing. I reach out, put my hand on the doorknob and try to twist it but it doesn't budge. Danvers must have gone home early. I turn and see Jack watching me from few feet away. He walks towards me and points to my chest.

"Use the key."

"What?"

"Use the key to open the door."

"Are you, Jack Hawkins, Model Student Extraordinaire suggesting I enter the principal's office while he is not there? I am shocked!"

He gives me a look that says 'well aren't you funny' and says. "Well yeah, but just to return the key. Nothing else."

"Right, but if I do that how are we supposed to lock the door when we come back out? I ask him, pulling my shoulders up and holding the palms of my hands out. He gears up to give a response but I raise my eyebrow at him, smiling.

"Okay, fair point. But just give it back soon, yes?"

"First thing tomorrow. I promise. Now come on let's go."

I push him in the chest and he turns and starts walking beside me, our arms brushing against each other. I slip my hand into Jack's. We walk down the stairs and I notice the store room that I hid in the other day, when I overheard Dave and Karen talking, is wide open, no one inside. No one in sight at all.

I shouldn't, should I? It would be a really bad idea. But there is no one around...

"You know, I think you are going to be a good influence on me."

"Well someone has to."

"But not too good I hope."

I raise my eyebrows and start to double back, Jack's hand still in mine.

"What are you doing?" He looks at me, confusion clouding his face.

I don't say anything. I just push him ahead of me into the store room, looking left and right down the corridor, to really make sure that no one is coming, that there is no chance of us being seen. When I am inside with Jack I close the door behind us. We are thrown into darkness. I look around me, blinking a few times, waiting for my eyes to adjust to the darkness. It doesn't take long until I can see an outline of Jack in front of me.

"Dean, what are you doing?"

I still say nothing. I reach out and pull Jack closer, until our noses are almost touching and put my lips on his. He kisses me back, his tongue making its way into my mouth, gently rolling over mine. I know it is taking a risk, that Jack will be likely to put a stop to it, say that we shouldn't be doing this in here, that I should show some responsibility. But there is no one around and I want to have some fun. And by the way he is kissing me now and feeling my body up through my uniform jumper it seems like he is definitely up for having some fun, like he isn't going to stop it. And as long as no one is around to catch us, I am up for it too.

I slip my bag off my shoulder. It falls onto the floor, making a dull clunking noise as it hits the floor. A second dull clunk on the floor tells me Jack has done the same with his. I put my hands on either side of his face and snake my fingers through his hair, feeling how soft and light it is against my fingertips. He pulls away from me, reaches down and starts to rub me through my trousers. I do the same and feel him, hard as a rock.

"Let's have sex." He sounds breathless, but excited.

"What, seriously?"

"Yes, seriously. Fuck me. Right here. I will show you that I am not, what did you call me earlier, Mr. Fun Sponge, wasn't it?."

CHAPTER TWENTY- TWO

Zoning Out

He unbuttons my trousers, pulls down the fly and tugs on them, bringing them down to rest at my ankles. I reach out and pull Jack's jumper up over his head, dumping it onto the floor. I fumble with the buttons on his shirt but it is too hard to undo them in the dark, not being able to see properly, so I pull it hard with both hands, ripping it open, the buttons shooting off in all different directions, clattering and pinging off things as they do. He drops it off, letting it fall from his shoulders and I start to kiss his neck, then make my way down his body, my lips and tounge gliding over his chest, his abs, his skin tasting so beautiful and sweet.

Jack drops his own trousers down and sinks to the floor, pulling me down on top of him. I grind on him, our hard cocks rubbing against each other, throbbing with each trust. I reach down and remove his trousers fully and slide in between his legs. I manouver myself into position and start to enter him but stop, hold my breath and raise my head, craning my neck towards the door. I think I heard something. Jack doesn't seem to have heard anything. He is pulling at my arms, wanting me to continue.

"Wait," I say to him, in a whisper. "Did you hear that?"

"Hear what?"

"Shush, there it is again. Fuck! I think someone's coming."

"Oh really? HELLOOOOOO!

"Shut up Jack!"

"Relax, there's no one there, now get back to business."

I feel the blood draining from all parts of me and listen for a minute but I don't hear anything. Maybe it is just in my head. There was no one around when we came in. The school was empty. Maybe the fear of getting caught is making me imagine things.

I lean forward and start to kiss his chest again but stop immediately. I definitely heard something that time. It was like a door closing or something. I can hear something else now, echoing. Like someone walking.

"Listen, is that footsteps?"

"Who cares?"

"Shut up Jack!"

"Come on, there's no one there, even if there is, who cares?"

"I fucking care. I don't want to get caught. "

I hear a third noise. Definitely the sound of someone walking through the corridor.

"That's footsteps. Jack you need to shut up! Please!"

Jack starts to speak, loud enough that if there is someone outside they will hear. Probably come investigate.

I feel myself start to panic, my chest starting to feel tight. This was a really stupid idea. I should not have started this. I should not have shown Jack the key. I should not have called him a fun sponge. Then he wouldn't have been trying to prove something. Then we wouldn't be on the verge of being seen like this.

And he fucking needs to shut up. Whoever is outside is bound to hear him. He won't stop talking. But if he does just shut up we might be clear, they might not come in here. It is only a store room. But if he keeps talking loudly they will and we will be in so much shit. I can feel the panic overtaking me so I fumble around on the floor, searching... for something. I grab the jumper from the floor and put it over his mouth. Just to keep him from talking. He taps my hand gently but I don't move it. I cannot let him make any noise. We cannot get caught.

He tries to say something but the sound is muffled by the jumper over his mouth. There's more footsteps outside, very close now. My heart is pounding so hard. It feels as if its about to burst out through my chest and flop around on the floor in front of me. Jack starts to buck underneath me but I press the jumper down harder and bring my knees up onto his bare chest, to keep him from moving. It works but I can still feel his body convulsing under me. I keep my eyes on the door, my ears straining for any sounds. I don't hear anything but, still, I don't move. I can't. If someone is outside and they come in here and catch us, our lives will be over. My parents will certainly make sure that I don't see the light of day ever again.

I shut my eyes, trying to force the thoughts of what my dad would do to me if he finds out, from my mind. They cannot find out. They just can't. And people at school can't find out either. What if it is a student out there and they open the door and see me and Jack naked together. Imagine the kind of hell Jimmy Browne would put me through, put *us* through. No, that can't happen. It can't. It just can't. We need to stay quiet until they pass. Until it is absolutely clear. Then we can get dressed and get the fuck out of here.

I wait for a while, my eyes closed but my ears still very much alert, listening for sounds outside. It seems quiet out there now. Thre are no more footsteps or echoes. My body relaxes slightly and I slide onto the floor beside Jack, letting out a long sigh.

"Fuu-uck, that was close." I can't help but let out a little nervous laugh, my chest rising and falling rapidly. "Imagine if we had been caught, I don't think I could have handled that."

I stand up, pull up my trousers, tuck my shirt in and straighten myself up. I can just about make out Jack still lying on the floor in the darkness.

"Come on," I say. "We need to get out of here."

He doesn't say anything. He doesn't make any effort to get up either. He is probably fuming. And I can't blame him. I have just had a complete over-reaction.

I kick his leg gently. "Jack, please don't be mad at me. We just couldn't get caught. So come on, get dressed, we need to leave."

He still makes no effort to get up. I can't fucking see him properly either, just a general outline of his body. I take a step back and fumble for the door knob opening the door a little. A sliver of light falls on him illuminating his naked body. He looks perfect, lying there, his arms by his sides. But he isn't looking at me. His eyes are closed.

"Come on Jack, stop messing, we really need to leave."

I stand over him and prod him gently on the shoulder with the tip of my foot. But he must be really mad at me, trying to trick me, because he isn't even opening his eyes.

"Jack seriously stop it. Get up"

Still nothing. I bend down and pull the jumper away from the bottom part of his face. He looks really still. I look down at his chest but it doesn't seem to be moving. No, that's not right. He can't-

"Jack? Jack?"

I say his name a few more times, my voice getting louder and more panicked each time. But he doesn't respond. I put my hands on either side of his face and shake his head. His eyes remain closed. I let go and his head lolls to one side, his eyes still closed, his mouth hanging open slightly. No- This is- It can't- No- Jack- He can't-

I scramble back and hit my head on a shelf behind me. Instinctively I reach up and rub my head, feeling something wet. I bring my hand in front of my eyes and see the tips of my fingers shining red. I rub it on the leg of my trousers, ignoring the stinging pain at the back of my head and look back down at Jack on the floor. Still. Unmoving.

No, no, no! Fuck! This cannot be happening. He can't be. I get down on my knees, grab him by the shoulders and shake him furiously. He is messing with me. Yeah, he has to be. Or he has just fainted. Yeah, he was shocked. And fainted. He will wake up in a second and we can have a good laugh about this. How funny it is that we nearly got caught and that the shock of it made him faint. We will be laughing about it all night. We have to.

I shake him again but he still doesn't move. No. Please. I put my head down close to his face, moving my ear in front of his mouth. I can't feel any breath coming out. I move down to his chest and press my ear up against it, leaving it there for a few seconds, waiting.

But I feel nothing.

Nothing.

CHAPTER TWENTY-THREE

Broken

No. No. No. Why is this happening? How is this happening? I feel my chest tightening, the air struggling to enter my lungs. I fall back onto my ass. I push myself backwards, scrambling, panicking, using my hands and feet to move. My back collides with something behind me. Probably the wall. Don't want to turn to see but I can't move any further. I put my head in between my legs and grip the back of my hair with both of my hands. Tears start to pour down my cheeks, hot and wet, falling fast. What the fuck have I done. I can't believe I've just- I can't – I have to-

I need to get out of here!

I try to stand but my legs buckle underneath me and I fall back into a heap on the floor, sobbing. I force myself to take a deep breath and push myself up onto my legs. They hold steady this time. I grab my bag up from the floor and make my way outside, standing with my back to the open door, looking frantically left and right down the empty corridor. I reach back, intending to close the door, but I can't do it. I can't just lock him in there, alone.

I can't. I need to leave it open. Someone needs to find him. So I pull it over, leaving it open a fraction, so that the room will not be in complete darkness.

I want to look back in at him, to see him again, but I can't bring myself to do it. I walk quickly through the corridor, turning into the main foyer, rushing out through the main door of the school, down the stone steps, almost losing my footing. But I stay on my feet and the air finally starts to enter my lungs as I head out through the still open gates of the school. I walk about twenty feet and break into a sprint, my legs working furiously to carry me away. I need to run. I just need to.

I run past Rykers Field. Past a pair of women who stare at me and shake their heads as I run, my arms swinging like crazy. Past a group of kids cycling on their push bikes, their laughter like a blender whirring inside my very skull. I pull my key out of my bag as I reach the end of the driveway in front of my house. I race up the concrete and insert it into the keyhole, twist it and push the door open. There's a rattling noise from the kitchen and my mum's voice calls out.

"Dean, is that you love?"

"Yeah." My voice comes out shaking, but barely a whisper. I swallow hard, steady my voice and speak again, louder. "Yeah, i-it's me Mum."

"What do you want to eat love."

"N-nothing Mum, I'm not hungry. I'm going up for a shower."

Her shadow passes close to the door and it starts to open inwards but I don't wait around. I can't let her see me in this state. I race up the stairs, almost tripping over each step, but steady myself using the banister. I fling my bag in through the open door of my bedroom and head straight for the bathroom. I lock the door and press my back up against it. A fresh wave of panic flows over me. My legs shake and my chest heaves.

What the fuck have I done? I left him there. I just left him there. What kind of fucking monster am I? What was I thinking. I should have stayed. I should have called someone. I should have done more to help. My stomach starts to turn and I sink to my knees, scrambling for the toilet. I lift the lid and throw my head into the bowl, just as a fountain of vomit surges up through my throat. It comes fast and thick, spraying the entire inside of the toilet bowl, slopping down the sides and coming to rest on top of the water.

I rest my head on the rim of the toilet bowl, the vomit still coming in little bursts, each one feeling like blades in my throat. I can't believe what's happening. I have killed someone. But not just *someone*. Jack. My Jack. I have killed him and I've left him. I start to bang my head against the rim of the toilet bowl but the pain is doing nothing. There is now only a tight knot in my chest. The rest of me is numb.

I wipe my mouth with the back of my hand, stand up and flush the toilet, washing away any remnants of vomit. I stagger over to the sink and hold on to the sides of it, griping the porcelain until my knuckles turn white and my fingers start to cramp. I don't even look up into the mirror. I can't. I can't look at myself. I turn the cold tap on and splash water up into my face. I don't even bother drying it off. I walk to the door and open it, walking slowly to my room, my feet feeling like two cinder blocks on the end of my legs. Closing the door behind me, I climb into my bed, clothes and shoes still on and pull the duvet up over me, covering my face completely.

A searing hot pain shoots across my temple and a picture of Jack, lying on the floor of that dark store room, flashes through my mind. I bring my hands up and rub both sides of my head, massaging my temples but it does nothing so I start to punch myself in the head using both my fists. I bring them down hard on my skull, my knuckles digging in deep. It's all my fault. I have fucked up so badly. There is no coming back from this. How am I supposed to live with myself now? I am a murderer. And I left him. I just fucking left him. Alone. Dead.

I turn on to my stomach and press my face into the pillow. I scream and scream, sobbing uncontrollably, the sounds barely audible, being absorbed by the thick fabric. I twist and turn, scraping and punching at the mattress with my hands. I fling the duvet cover off me and stare up at the ceiling. I turn my head to the left and see my laptop on top of my desk, the cover not fully closed. I swing my legs over the side of the bed, stand up and grab the laptop from my desk. I don't go back to the bed, instead just letting myself sink onto the floor in front of my desk where I open up the laptop fully. I power it on and the homescreen pops up, all of the little icons blinking into existence.

The internal fan of the laptop starts to whirr and I hover my finger over the mouse pad. I don't even know why I turned this stupid thing on. It can't help me right now. I slide my finger over the mousepad watching as the little cursor on the screen shoots towards the browser icon. I double click it and the browser pops open on the screen. I click on the 'Bookmarks' tab and scroll down the list until I reach the J's. There it is. But I can't click it yet. I need a minute.

I give another double click on the mousepad and it

springs up onto the screen. Jack Hawkins' Facebook profile. I click on the profile picture and it fills the screen. He is smiling, happy, full of life. But he is none of those things any more. He never will be again. And all because of me. A hot tear slides down my cheek. Look at his beautiful eyes, his perfect lips. I remember how good they felt. But I will never get to see them again, never get to kiss them again, never get to be happy again.

I reach up and touch the picture of Jack, my finger trembling. I try to speak but the words don't come. My lips just move silently in the shape of the words 'I'm sorry.' I push the top cover of the laptop back until I hear the plastic begin to crack. I bend it backwards over my knee and the screen goes blank, a rectangle of blackness and nothing. I stand up and force it further backwards until the outsides of the top and bottom are touching. I pull it every which way I can until the wires are exposed and all that is left is the two halves of the laptop in either hand.

I swing them around, bring them up and crashing back down until they are bouncing off the desk in front of me, the vibrations reverberating through my hands. The letters from the keyboard come flying off and scatter all over the foor. Pieces of plastic spit in every direction. I fling the half of the laptop in my right hand away from me first. It crashes into my wardrobe with an almighty thud. The piece in my left hand goes next, colling with the wall near the door.

Frantic footsteps come thumping up the stairs and my dad's voice booms, like thunder. I didn't even know he was here. I didn't notice the car in the driveway on my way in. Not that I was paying much attention anyway.

"Dean, what is all the racket, what the hell are you

doing in there?"

I run to the door and push my two hands up against it, palms flat on the wood, my fingers splayed. My dad pushes down on the handle, trying to open it, but I hold my position and it snaps shut. I plant my feet more firmly on the ground and brace for another push. It comes but I hold steady again and it opens even less this time and snaps shut once more.

"Dean, open this fucking door!"

"No."

He pushes again but it barely budges this time.

"Dean. I am telling you! Open this door right now, or so help me God, I will fucking break it down!"

"No. Just fuck off and leave me alone!"

"Don't you dare speak to me like that. Open this door right now!"

"No. Just get the fuck away from me!"

I expect another, more fierce push to come but it doesn't. I hear my dad, sigh, grunt, then turn and walk away, his footsteps heavy but deliberate. I stay in my defensive position and the sound of voices float up from downstairs. First my dad's then my mum's. I can't make out any words. But they are becoming more raised, the intensity in them growing. There are footsteps on the stairs again but softer this time. Definitely my mum. A few seconds later there is a tap at the door. I don't say anything. Another even gentler tap comes and then my mum calls out.

"Dean, love, will you open the door please? There's food downstairs for you, come down and eat it."

"I'm not hungry."

"Why not love, what's wrong?"

"Nothing, Mum, Jesus! I'm just not hungry. So just leave

me alone please. I don't want to talk to anyone right now." My voice is shaking like crazy and I fight to hold back the sobs. I hear my mum sighing on the other side of the door.

"Okay, love, well when you are ready to talk I'll just be downstairs."

But there is no sound of her footsteps retreating, so it's obvious she is lingering outside, listening, maybe has her ear pressed up against the door. I stay as still as I can, my hands still pressed up against the wood. After a few minutes I hear her shuffling away, her footsteps slow on the stairs. My hands slide away from the door and I drop to the floor where I am.

I pull myself into the foetal position, my back against the door in case anyone tries to open it and stare ahead of me, at the leg of my bed. After a while the room becomes dark around me and I can see nothing but dark outlines. But I still just stare forward, sobbing silently now, feeling broken.

CHAPTER TWENTY- FOUR

Falling Apart

I must have fallen asleep because I open my eyes and they sting. I don't remember drifting off though. All I remember is shifting my body around all night just staring out into the darkness, the thoughts of what has happened, of what I have done, whizzing through my brain. I blink a few times, trying to get my eyes adjusted to the light streaming in through my window. There is dried drool on my chin. I try to lift my head up from the floor but I can't, so I turn onto my back, rub my eyes with the palms of my hands and stare up at the ceiling. My back is starting to ache from being on the floor all night so I force myself to lift my head from the floor and hoist myself up into a sitting position. I look over at the clock on my bedside table. 7:59 am.

I stand up, pick up my phone and key, stick them into my trouser pockets and sit on the edge of my bed, chew ingon my bottom lip and rubbing my legs, tyring to think what to do. I stand up again and make my way out onto the landing. There are no sounds, the house eerily quiet. Darren's bedroom door is still closed. So he must still be sleeping. I heard him coming in pretty late last night, swearing as he knocked over the vase on the landing and fumbled to put it back in place. But my mum and dad's bedroom door is slightly ajar, so one or both of them must be up. I plod silently down the stairs and head straight for the kitchen. My dad is sitting at the table, a mug with steam rising from the top of it set out in front of him, his phone flat on the tabe beside that, face down. I turn my head away from him, not giving him a chance to see my face, open the fridge and take a swig of milk from the almost empty carton.

"Well?" His tone is stern.

I don't look at him. I can't right now. I just put the carton back into the fridge and walk back out into the hallway. I reach the front door, pull it open and step out into the driveway, closing it gently behind me. My eyes sting and my head aches like crazy but I need to just keep moving. Not because I want to but because I have to. I have to get to school. I have to get back to Jack.

I walk slowly, trying not to think of what I've done but failing miserably. It is all I can think about. I have fucked up so badly. There are no words to describe this situation. I have killed someone. I mean I have actually stopped someone from living. That is beyond fucked up. I didn't mean for it to happen. But it did. And it is my fault. I chose to go into the store room. I chose to put the jumper over his face, just to keep him quiet, just to stop us from being caught. What was I thinking? He must have been panicking so much, but I was too concerned with getting caught that I was oblivious to it. I was so caught up in my own mind that I didn't even notice I was killing him, didn't even notice I was crushing the air out of him.

Fresh tears are rolling down my face but I wipe them away with my shaking hand. I just need to go back to him and get some help. I need to go in and raise the alarm. I can just say I found him like that. No one will know that it was me. There is nothing to link us. Nothing to say that I was in that store room with him...

I turn the corner and start to head for the school, but a large crowd in the middle of the road and the sight of blue flashing lights over the heads of the people stop me dead in my tracks. No, no, no. Fuck! I am too late. Someone must have found him already. This is not good. I need to think.

I raise both my hands and run them through my hair. There's a sharp stinging sensation as they pass over the back of my head. I feel around with the fingers of my right hand and they come to rest on a small cut. Shit! No! I forgot about cutting my head when I hit it. I look down and see the dried smear of blood on the leg of my trousers where I wiped the blood from my fingers.

I lick my fingers and try to wipe the blood off my trousers but it makes no difference. The stain stays where it is, reminding me what a colossal mess I have made of everything. They are going to find my blood in that store room. On whatever I banged my head off. I don't even fucking know what it was. It was too dark. But they are going to find it. They will know it was me. They will come for me. They will lock me up.

My chest starts to tighten but I force myself to breathe deeply, to inhale large gulps of oxygen. I can't panic. Not here. Not in the open. I need to get away before-

"Oh my God, Dean, what's going on?"

I freeze, my breath catching in my throat. I turn my head slightly to the left as someone walks up behind me, draws level with me and comes to a stop. Karen looks at me quizzically then looks back at the crowd gathered in front of the school gates.

"Oh, er, hi Karen." I try to keep my voice calm, my tone neutral, but it's impossible to even gauge how successful I am. "I've no idea what's going on. I just got here."

"You don't think someone got hurt do you? There are police cars *and* an ambulance."

"Oh, I dunno, maybe."

Jesus! I could not sound any more stupid if I tried. I don't know what to say. But I need to just feign ignorance, play along. For now at least.

"Come on, let's go closer. I'm gonna text Dave, tell him to hurry up." Karen pulls her phone out and her fingers move rapidly across the screen of her phone.

We walk slowly together, embedding ourselves into the crowd of people. Inside the gates of the school, parked close to the stone steps is an ambulance and one police car. Outside there are a further two police cars, flanking the gates. Two traffic cones stand beside each one and a band of "POLICE- DO NOT CROSS" tape is stretched between them. Police officers in their uniforms, their faces blank, their hands stuffed into their jacket pockets, stand just in front of the crowd, blocking entry into the school grounds. The people around us are talking animatedly, all of them wondering what is happening. But I don't need to wonder. I know exactly what is going on.

I want to turn and run because I know exactly what is going to happen. And although I am aware that Karen is talking to me, I am not even registering what it is she is saying. So I just nod and grumble anyway, hopefully not looking too suspicious. I feel someone pat me on the back and turn to see Dave, my oldest and best friend in the world sidle in beside me and Karen and take her hand into his.

"Anyone know what happened?" He stands on the tips of his toes, peering over the heads of everyone in front of him.

"No idea," I say. "Maybe someone had an accident or something."

"Fuck me, is that...?" Dave doesn't finish his question. "Holy shit. It is. Look."

I look up at Dave's face, seeing shock and confusion spread across it. Karen strains her neck looking past the people in front of her and lets out an audible gasp as do many of the people around us. My stomach start to churn. Because I know what they are seeing. I know why the ambulance is there. I know that they are watching the paramedics wheel a trolley out. A trolley with a sealed, black body bag on top, Jack's corpse inside.

I look past the shoulder of the woman standing in front of me and watch as the two paramedics load the trolley into the back of the ambulance, their faces sullen. Two police officers walk down the stone steps followed by Mr. Danvers and a woman I recognise as being one of the cleaners of the school. Mr Danvers has his arm around her shoulders. Both of them look as if they are about to collapse onto the ground. My stomach churns again and I feel something starting to rise up through my oesophagus.

Without saying anything to Dave and Karen, who are still staring, wide eyed, at the events unfolding in front of them I turn and make my way quickly through the crowd. The amount of people standing around seems to have tripled in the few minutes we have been standing here. I think I can hear Dave's voice calling behind me but I move on and burst out through the throng of people, taking off furiously down the street, my legs working frantically to get me away.

I turn left onto a side street and slow down to a jog. I come to a stop and bend over, my hands resting on my knees. I heave and a fresh wave of vomit comes spewing from my mouth. It splatters onto the ground at my feet and I start to sob uncontrollably.

CHAPTER TWENTY- FIVE

Spying

I stand up straight, wipe my mouth with the back of my sleeve and walk, leaving the pool of chunky vomit on the concerete behind me. I walk aimlessly, oblivious to everything and everyone that passes. I keep my head bowed, afraid to look up in case anyone sees what a state I am in and tries to help. Not that they could do much for me anyway. I am truly fucked. I don't know how I am going to live with myself. My head is pounding and every time I get an image of Jack in my head it is as if I am being stabbed through the heart with a blade of ice.

I stuff my hands into my pockets and just let my legs carry me. I don't want to stay still. I can't. I need to keep moving. I don't know where to, but I just know I have to keep going. I need time to think. About Jack. About everything that has happened. About how I am going to get myself out of this horrendous shit show. Because they are going to find my blood in that store room before too long. Because the police won't hesitate in trying to find out whose blood it is, as soon as they have determined that it isn't Jack's. Because when they find out that it is my blood and that I was in that store room, with Jack, I am going to have to confess. To everything. But I don't know if I have the strength for that. For people to know everything. For people to know how much of a monster I am.

I look up, finding myself turning round a corner onto a street full of houses. I haven't been paying attention to where my legs have been taking me, but, looking at the familiar rows of houses, I realise I am just a couple of streets over from the street that Jack's house is on. A police car comes whizzing past me and I quicken my strides, following it, confident of its destination.

I reach the end of the street just as the police car pulls to a stop outside the driveway in front of Jack's house. It sits there for a minute and I stand still, watching. Two police officers step out of their car, one male and one female. They place their caps on their heads, straighten them, give each other a brief nod and begin their walk up Jack's driveway. I duck in behind a bush in front of a house near where I'm standing. But I make sure I still have a clear view the two police officers as they reach the door of Jack's house.

The female police officer reaches up and raps on the door with the knuckles of her outstretched arm, while her colleague stands straight-backed, with his hands behind his back. She raises her hand once more, getting ready to knock on the door again but she stops mid air when he door swings open. Even though it is too far away to see things in great detail, I see the expression on Jack's mum's face change as she takes in the image of the two police officers standing in front of her, her smile slipping, replaced by a look of concern.

They remove their hats and hold them in front of their

jacketed bodies as the female officer speaks, the words inaudible to me from this distance. Mrs. Hawkins sways in the doorway and the male police officer reaches out just in time to catch her as she falls forward. He pulls her up and steadies her, while she grabs for the door handle with one hand, her other one cupping her face. She turns around and moves slowly, unsteadily, into the house. The two police officers follow, closing the door behind them.

I stand in place, frozen to the spot, warm tears trickling down my face. I shouldn't have returned here. I shouldn't have spied on the moment that the police officers told Mrs. Hawkins that her son is dead. That they found his body, lying naked and alone in the store room of his school. Although I am feeling pain at having done it, it must be only a fraction of the pain that Mrs. Hawkins is now feeling, having lost her only son. And it is all my fault.

As I am wiping the tears fom my cheeks with the ends of my sleeves, the door of the house opens and the three people emerge. Mrs. Hawkin's is wearing her coat now and sobbing. Deep, heavy sobs. The female officer has her arm around her and walks her slowly down the driveway, taking careful steps. The male officer slams the door of the house shut behind him and walks out into the street, darting ahead of the two women. He opens the back passenger door of the patrol car and the female officer guides Mrs' Hawkins into it, closing it gently as she settles in. She then walks around to the other side of the car and slides into the back beside the distraught mother. The male officer gets into the front driver's seat. I hear the engine flare to life and the screech of tyres on the concrete as they drive away with speed.

I press myself into the bush as they pass by me, holding my breath and closing my eyes tight, hoping that they do not glance out of the window and see me.

CHAPTER TWENTY- SIX

Rykers Field

I breathe out slowly, twigs and leaves from the bush poking at me from every angle. I shouldn't have come here. I shouldn't have spied something so devastating, on the moment that a mother found out her son is no longer in this world. I need to get get away from here. To think about what I can do. So I pull myself out of the bush and walk, with purpose this time, a destination- home- in mind.

I decide to take the shortest route to get there- the one that passes by Rykers Field. There are a group of people in the distance passing by one of the old, netless goalposts. One of the figures, the shortest of them, turns and jumps into the air, grabbing for the crossbar, the rest watching him. He misses, his fingers just grazing off the bottom of the metal bar. The others around him all laugh and guffaw as he lands on his back. As I get closer to them I see that it is Jimmy Browne with his gang of morons in tow. They must be on their way back from the school. Jimmy's voice rings out above everyone else's, making the hairs on the back of my neck bristle and anger rise inside me.

"You'd wanna watch yourself Nato, if you fall like that again you'll end up brown bread like that idiot at the scool."

The whole gang of wasters laugh at this and I immediately change course, veering off the footpath and onto the grass, heading straight for them. The one called Nato hauls himself up from the ground and I hear Jenny Crawley's voice asking something about 'who everyone thinks it is', but no one answers her. Everyone is staring at me as I make my way towards them. Jimmy is starting to mouth off again, but I don't pay any attention to what he is saying. I stare him dead in the eyes, walk up to him and push him full force in the chest. He stumbles backwards and looks in complete shock as he trips over his own feet and lands flat on his back in the grass.

"Think it's funny to make jokes about someone who's dead do you?" I scream at him, venom attached to every word and every syllable that comes shooting out of my mouth. "You think you're such a funny cunt, don't you? But you're not, you're just pure scum."

The look of shock on his face is replaced with one of fury and he scrambles quickly to his feet. He pulls his schoolbag from his back and throws it to the ground. He balls both of his hands into fists as his gang starts to close in around me, each of them flinging their own schoolbags onto the ground, sneers on their faces, looking ready to pounce on me.

Jimmy shakes his head at them as if to say 'leave him to me' and they back off just a little, but stay in tight formation, leaving no gap for me to escape through. Bu, that's fine. I'm not going to run. No way! I have had enough of Jimmy Browne. And making a joke about someone who was found dead in the school is going too far. It doesn't even matter that it is Jack, it is just disgusting.

"Well, come on then, you little poof, don't start a fight if you're not going to finish it," Jimmy growls at me, raising both his balled fists and inching towards me.

I stand absolutely no chance against this animal. He is going to destroy me, I know it. Fighting and violence comes second nature to someone like Jimmy Browne. But, if I can just get one good punch in, I will be satisfied. So, taking a risk, I lunge at him, my right hand flying through the air. But he sidesteps, dodging my punch. I see his fist arch up and feel it connect with my jaw. I try to stumble backwards out of his reach but another of his punches lands on my ribs.

I raise my arms up to protect my face, close my eyes and feel Jimmy lay into me again and again, punches connecting with every available space on my body. Something collides with the back of my left leg and it buckles underneath me, sending me face first onto the muddy grass. There are several kicks coming at me now, not just from Jimmy anymore, all at the same time. So I curl up into a ball to protect myself as much as possible, taking most of the blows to my back, ribs and legs, each blow feeling just as bad, if not worse, as the last.

The kicks stop and a hand grabs the front of my jumper, pulling me up. I open my eyes and see Jimmy's face, just centimetres from mine, his expression one of pure evil.

"Don't ever fucking start something you can't finish, you little poof."

I don't say anything, just stare into Jimmy's eyes, waiting for him to start punching me again while I'm at his disposal. But he doesn't. Instead, he releases his grip and stands up straight.

He moves away from me and beckons to the rest of his gang to follow. "Come on," he says to them. "This little poof isn't worth it."

I hear them all laughing as they pick up their bags from the grass. The sound of their voices grows fainter as the group of teenagers gets further away and I turn onto my back, grimacing, as searing hot pain shoots through every inch of my body, my back hurting like hell and my ribs feeling as if they have been cracked wide open. I sit up, groaning in pain as I do and wipe my face with the bottom of my jumper. It comes away muddy but relatively blood free.

You could say I'm lucky, I guess, that most of the blows struck my body and missed out my face. But I wish they hadn't. I wish they had got my face, my head. I wish they had beaten me to death.

A monster like me deserves it.

CHAPTER TWENTY-SEVEN

In The Bath

Dad's car isn't in the driveway and there are no windows open at the front of the house, so I don't think anyone is at home. But still, I push my key into the lock quietly, trying to make no sound, just in case. I can't let anyone see me in this state. I don't know how I look, but it probably isn't great. My jaw feels swollen and pain shoots through me with every step I take. I close the door softly, making as little noise as possible and head straight up the stairs, each step becoming more arduous as I climb. My hand clings on to the banister tightly.

I head straight into the bathroom and lock the door behind me. I look at myself in the mirror for the first time in days and take a step back, in shock. It is dreadful. My hair is unkempt and greasy, my eyes look red and swollen but somehow sunken into my skull at the same time and there is a slight bruise beginning to appear on my puffed up jaw where Jimmy's first punch landed.

I pull my jumper up over my head, grittting my teeth at the pain that flares up in my body as I move my hands up into the air. I toss it onto the tiled floor and take off the rest of my clothes, leaving them in a ragged pile. My phone rests on top, a long crack visible on the screen. I don't even care. It can stay broken.

Turning around I climb awkwardly into the bath, the porcelain feeling cold against my flesh. I lean forward, put the stopper in and turn on one of the taps, laying back as the pipes gurgle and water splashes in, filling up the bath tub.

The icy cold water touches my bare skin as it begins to surround me. But I don't care that it's cold. I just lay back, resting my head on the end of the bath letting the water rise up around me. I breathe deeply, my ribs aching with each breath, my lungs expanding into the pain. I wait for the bath to be as full as it possibly can, the water coming up as far as the overflow hole and turn off the tap with my foot. It flops back down into the water, the water rippling around it.

I close my eyes and think about Mrs. Hawkins. How she looked as the officers told her that her son is dead. How she was cradled and propped up by the female police officer as she was led to the car, obviously to be brought to the morgue to make a formal identification of the body. I picture her standing by as the coroner pulls the sheet down and reveals the corpse of her son. I picture her sobbing, barely able to stand, probably still being propped up by the female officer as she confirms that, yes it is her son, lying still, dead and cold on that clinical slab.

She must feel like her whole world has collapsed around her. First her husband, now her son, both taken from her at such young ages. And it is all my fault. All my fault. I don't deserve to live. It isn't fair that he is dead, while I'm still here, still breathing, still alive. He was a far better person than I will ever be. But now no one will ever know that. I have taken that away.

I hold my breath and, sliding down in the bath, plunge my head straight under the water. Instinctively my mouth closes and I hold my breath. But I don't want that. I don't want to live, knowing that I have killed someone, knowing that I left him there, still and unmoving on that dirty floor. I don't want to live without Jack.

I open my mouth and inhale deeply, feeling the water enter my lungs. My chest tightens and constricts, trying to fight back against me. I hold my head under, wanting the water to fill me up, to take me. But my hands and feet start to thrash and I sit up, my head breaking through the surface of the water, coughing and spluttering, my body trying to expel the water out of my body.

I cough again, water falling from my mouth into the murky water. I slick my hair back out of my eyes and rub my face with both hands, sighing, realising how stupid I have just been. Stupid to think I can drown myself in my own bath tub. It's obvious that an innate instinct to survive would kick in as soon as I tried. But I am not thinking clearly. My head is just completely fucked up right now.

I sit in the cold water for another few minutes, then reach down and pull out the stopper, listening as the water vacates the bath tub, swirling and swishing, travelling swiftly through the pipes. I stand up, my body still extremely sore, step out onto the mat on the floor beside the bath tub and grab a towel from the rail over the radiator. I towel myself dry, carefully, not pressing too hard on any part of me that feels too tender. There is bruising starting to appear on my chest and on my legs.

I finish drying my hair, drop the towel into the now

empty bath tub and grab my pile of clothes from the floor, my phone wobbling on top as I balance the pile in one hand, my other grabbing the handle, opening the door. I cross the landing, feeling a draught on my naked ass and make my way into my room. I toss my phone and keys onto my desk and look at the bundle of clothes in my arms. I sniff them and recoil a little. They stink of mud and sweat. They even look filthy too. I move the chair away from the desk, bend and extract the rubbish bin that I haven't emptied in weeks from underneath it. I stuff the dirty pile of clothes into it and shove it back under.

I sit on the edge of the chair in front of my desk, cradling my ribs as I settle in and fumble around in the drawer nearest to me on my left, pulling out a navy t-shirt and a pair of shorts. I slip them on slowly and relax back into the chair. I grab my phone from the desk and press the home button. It lights up so I slide my finger across the screen, dragging the little lock symbol from one side to the other. It moves without hesitation, so the crack hasn't damaged it too badly then. It still works, even if the image is a little distorted. I pull down the no-tification tab and immediately see several notifications, mostly text messages and facebook notifications. But I slide them all across, clearing them from the screen.

I don't clear the last one though. I tap on it and it brings me to Facebook. There are a million and one posts popping up on my newsfeed from my friends and classmates, a new one popping up every few seconds, all concerned with one thing, all asking the same question. Comment after comment pops up under each post.

OH MY GOD! I cannot believe it.

A dead body at our school!

Did you see who it was? Did anyone see who it was?

I hope its not Lennon. He is FINE!

The school will have to close.

Fuck Yes! Time off!

I stop reading the posts and comments, the repetitiveness and lack of empathy starting to annoy me. My phone starts to vibrate and Dave's name pops up on the screen. My heart lurches up into my throat but I decline the call. A few seconds later a message from Karen pops up but I swipe it off the screen before I can see what it says. I press and hold down the power button until the screen goes black.

CHAPTER TWENTY- EIGHT

At Jack's Again

It is Thursday. Morning, but I don't know the exact time. Still in bed. Still aching all over. My mum almost fainted when she came in yesterday afternoon and found me in such a state. After her initial shock she demanded to know what happened, insisting that I should go to the hospital. But I told her no. No hospitals. I told her I slipped down the stone steps outside the school and that it didn't hurt that much. It is a weak excuse, I know, but it was all I could think of on the spot. And she definitely doesn't believe it, I could see it in her eyes. But she didn't question it.

I lay in bed as she brought up food, drinks and pain-killers all evening, every time saying that I should think about going to the hospital, but I just kept refusing. Then at around eight o'clock she came running up the stairs to tell me she received an alert from the school. She had tears in her eyes as she passed me the phone so I could read the message. It said that a tragic accident had oc-cured and that a student had died on the premises and that the school would be closed for the remainder of the week and possibly longer as investigations take place. The message didn't mention who the student was, which I'm glad of, because I don't think I could have held back the sobs as successfully as I did if I had seen Jack's name on the screen.

"Oh my lord, it is absolutely terrible," my mum had uttered through her fingers, which she had clasped over her mouth.

She went back downstairs after our brief conversation and left me alone in my room. I lay awake most of the night staring up at the ceiling as the room grew dark around me. I thought several times about rushing downstairs and telling my mum and dad about everything. But I didn't. I can't. Probably because I haven't got the strength to admit it. But really probably because I am broken. And afraid. My mind was racing, trying but failing to think of a way to deal with this whole situation, wishing that I could turn back time so that none of it had ever happened. Wishing that it wouldn't hurt as much as it does.

Darren came home and popped his head around my door around midnight. I didn't ask where he was coming from. Didn't care. He looked at me suspiciously when I regaled him with the fake story about falling down the steps at school. He doesn't believe a word of it.

"Nah," he said to me, shaking his head and scrunching up his nose. "Not true. I've been in enough fights to know what those types of injuries look like. You might be able to fool Mum, but there's no way you're getting that bullshit past me."

I just turned my head away from him and stared blankly at the wall, saying nothing.

"You don't get to lie to me," he continued. "You know

that. Whatever issues you have about telling Mum what happened to you is one thing. But you do not get to lie to me. I want the truth, Beanie, Now."

My eyes started to sting then and I felt hot tears forming at the corners, so I forced them shut and just whispered "I don't wanna talk about it. Just drop it."

I don't know if he heard me or not because he didn't say anything further. He just withdrew from my room, crossed the landing and went into his own room.

Now I lift myself into a sitting position, my entire body feeling sore and exhausted. I wince as I swing my legs out of bed and stand, clutching my ribs. I pull some fresh clothes out of my wardrobe and struggle to change into them . My phone is sitting face down on top of my desk. I should probably check it. There are probably a bundle of messages and missed calls. But I don't want to. I don't feel like speaking to anyone. I don't think I will ever feel like speaking to anyone again.

I grab my key and stuff it into my trouser pocket, slip my shoes on and make my way down to the kitchen. My mum is standing by the sink, her phone pressed to her ear, her expression sad. She gestures for me to sit at the table. As she talks, her phone held up with one hand, she puts a glass and plate in front of me with the other. She takes some bread out and puts it into the toaster. While the bread is cooking, she pours some orange juice into the glass and puts the tub of painkillers in front of me. I pop two out and swallow them, washing them down with the cold juice.

She continues talking on the phone but it's difficult to discern exactly what she's talking about. I am only hearing one side of the conversation and it is mainly just a bunch of 'Yesses' and 'Nos'. When the toast pops up she grabs it out with the tips of her fingers and places the two slices on the plate in front of me. I butter them slowly and watch as the butter melts. I'm not really hungry. I'm not really anything right now, but I eat anyway.

My mum hangs up her phone, puts it down on the counter top and sits at the table beside me. "That was your Aunt Sharon. She heard about the body being found at the school and just wanted to check in."

"That's nice of her," I say. "But how did she find out. She lives miles away."

"She said it was on the news apparently."

"Oh."

Fuck! I hadn't even thought of the fact that it would be on the news. I swallow the soggy piece of toast in my mouth and push the other slice towards my mum. I can't finish it now. I feel ill.

"Here, you can have this Mum, I'm not hungry."

"Okay love, are you feeling okay? Did you take some more painkillers?"

"Yeah, Mum, I took two just now." I stand up slowly and push my chair in. "I'm heading out. I'm gonna go to Dave's house."

She looks at me suspiciously. "Are you sure love? You're not really in any shape to be going anywhere."

"Yeah, I'm fine Mum. I won't be long."

"Okay, just be careful son."

I make my way out of kitchen and into the hallway. I hear my mum's chair scrape on the floor and her foot-steps behind me.

"Dean."

I freeze, my hand on the door handle. I half turn back to face my mum and she is standing in the doorway, her left hand gripping the frame of the door very tightly.

"Yeah Mum?

"Dean, I'm only going to ask you once and I want you to be honest with me love, because I'm your mum and I love you and I will protect you no matter what." Her voice is shaking and I can sense where this is going. I really wish she wouldn't. "Do your injuries have anything at all to do with that body being found at the school?"

I should tell her. I should come clean now, while I can. While she is giving me the opportunity. Before it is too late. Before things escalate out of everyone's control. But I can't. I can't admit it, can't face it. I open the door, turn my head away from her and take a deep breath, making my voice steady as a rock.

"No, Mum. I told you already. I fell down the steps at school."

I told my mum I was going to Dave's house. But that is not true. I don't know where I'm going. I just know that I can't sit around at home. Especially not with my mum being there. She would be hovering around me all day, probably insist, again, that I go to the hospital, probably try to weed the truth out of me. So no, staying at home right now is not an option. But I can't just go to Dave's either. I don't think I would be able to hide anything from him. He would be able to get me to tell the truth.

So, I turn left, walk sullenly and then eventually turn right, onto Jack's street. But it isn't Jack's street anymore is it? It never will be his steet again. And I definitely shouldn't even be coming here, but I have nowhere else to go.

I reach Jack's house, noticing that there are two cars

parked in the driveway, and a load more parked on the street. I am not sure if they have always been there, whether they belong to the residents of this street or they are new. I never took much notice of before.

I walk up and stand outside the driveway. The drapes both upstairs and downstairs are closed, making the house look even more forlorn than it already is. If the two cars weren't parked in the driveway, you would think that the house was derelict, abandoned, just an empty shell.

I reach out and put my hand on the gate and start to push it open, to walk up the driveway, but I freeze. I can't do it. I want to, but I can't. Can't face the thought of standing where he would have stood, of being where he would have been. I can't bear the thought of being face to face with Mrs. Hawkins, knowing what I have done to her son, knowing how much pain I have caused for her and her family.

My chest tightens and my breath catches in my throat. I sway on the spot and then turn and run, hearing the gate swing closed with a clang behind me.

CHAPTER TWENTY- NINE

Asking For Help

My feet slap the concrete hard as I run. I don't even know why I'm running or where I'm running to. I don't know anything anymore. I don't know what to feel, what to think, what to do. I am really falling apart, unravelling completely. All I do know is that I am a monster. A sick, murderous monster who doesn't deserve to live, who deserves ten times the amount of pain that I am already feeling in my ribs and heart as I take each breath.

I lift my head and slow down to a walking pace as I see a flash of railing ahead of me. The old distillery. I take a deep breath and walk towards it. I slip in through the familiar gap and close my eyes as I move forward, my feet crunching on the gravel underfoot.

I stop when I reach the spot that Jack first kissed me and I punched him, sending him sprawling to the ground. I remember feeling so confused and wondering why, for the few seconds that I kissed him back, it felt so natural. But now, now I wish that Jack was here with me. I wish that I could kiss him just one more time, tell him how much I ws starting to care about him, tell him how comfortable I was beginning to feel with him.

I move on, making my way around the side of the old building. I sit on the ground, my back pressed up against the brick wall, my legs drawn up to my chest. I bury my face in my knees and think about how I sat here with Jack, just last week and how we kissed properly and how it felt so mind-blowingly good.

I thrust my head back and smash it into the wall, gritting my teeth at the pain. Fucking pain. I stand up and face the wall. I take a deep breath and scream, an incoherent jumble of sounds, my right hand balling into a fist. The sound of my scream echoes throughout the empty grounds and I bring my fist up and punch the wall. I punch it a second time. A third. Fourth. I punch it until my knuckles are bloody and it feels as if my hand is about to fall off.

I raise my my right, bloodied hand in front of me and hold it with my left. I cannot keep going on like this. It is too much. The pain inside of me is too much. I need to tell someone what I did. I need to ask for help.

I pace up and down my room, the door wide open, listening, waiting for the front door downstairs to open, for him to step into the hallway so that I can grab him quickly, before he does anything else. Because I have to tell him. I have to. He will know what to do. He will be able to help.

I look at the clock on my bedside table and let out a deep sigh. He is taking fucking ages. If he doesn't get home soon, I will end up talking myself out of it, I won't be able to ask fo-

The front door downstairs opens and closes. I race out onto the landing and stand at the top of the stairs.

"Darren!"

He pops his head over the banister and looks up at me.

"Yo, Beanie, whats up?"

"I need to talk to you."

"Right, I'll be up in a sec, just lemme get something to eat first." He starts to turn his head away from me.

"No!" The sound of my voice is sharp, harsh. "I need to talk to you now. It's fucking important."

He snaps his head back in my direction, his eyes narrowed.

"Now" I say, staring him dead in the eyes, my expression serious, grim.

He takes the stairs two at a time and is standing in front of me in a matter of seconds. He regards me suspiciously for a moment but sees the expression on my face. He knows I am not kidding. He walks past me into his own bedroom and I follow him quickly. He stands at the door and waits for me to pass him. He closes the door firmly when the both of us are inside the room. He slides past me and sits on the small armchair beside his bed, removing things from his pockets and dumping them on the bed, where they make a small imprint on the puffed up covers.

"What's going on? What's so urgent?"

I move in front of him, then back, pacing from side to side, keeping my head bowed. I need to tell him but I don't know how to say it. I don't know what words to use, how to explain it. I open my mouth, gearing myself up to start talking, but close it again wen the words don't come.

"Dean, what the fuck? Just spit it out."

I take a deep breath, stop moving and look at him. "I fucked up, I really, really fucked up" I say quickly, hoping that he will grasp some meaning from what I am saying. "I did it. It was me."

"Did it? Did what? What was you?" He leans back in his chair, pulls his shoulders up around his ears and shakes his head. "Dean, you're not making any sense."

I feel my eyes start to water and my chest start to constrict. He doesn't understand. He doesn't get it. Fuck! I just need to say it.

"I killed him," I say, my legs starting to wobble underneath me. But I tense them, forcing myself to stay upright. "I killed Jack."

"What are you talking about Dean? What do you mean you killed Jack? Jack who?"

"Jack Jack Hawkins the body they found at the school I did it and I left him there but I didn't mean to it was an accident I loved him Darren but I killed him and I just feel empty and I'm freaking out and I don't know what to do help me please."

I'm talking fast, the words almost colliding with each other as they leave my mouth. But I have to talk fast. Because I have said it now and I need him to hear it. I need him to tell me what to do. He stares up at me blankly from his seated position, saying nothing. I feel tears flowing down my cheeks, hot and wet.

"I fucking killed him Darren," I say again, quieter this time, realising, truly, the enormity of what I have done.

My chest heaves and my legs wobble fiercely. I fight to stay standing but they give out and I feel myself sinking to the floor, my eyes falling shut and my sobs coming now, fierce, uncontrollably. I feel Darren move swiftly from his chair and wrap his arms around me. I lean into his chest. He is shaking.

"It's okay," he says and I feel his head nodding. "It's okay. We will sort this." He grabs my face and I look into his eyes. He looks afraid but he doesn't blink, doesn't waver. "We will sort this, Dean. I promise."

Eventually, after I don't know how long, Darren stands, pulling me up with him. I wipe my eyes with the back of my hand, my damaged knuckles stinging as the salty tears make contact. Darren turns away from me and I see his hand going up to his face, wiping his eyes. He turns back to me, his face serious.

"I'm going to help you, Dean. But I need to know exactly what happened."

I swallow hard and tell him. I tell him how I brought Jack into the store room, that we started to mess around, that I thought I heard footsteps outside, that I tried to keep Jack from making noise but I didn't realise that I was cutting off his air supply. How I panicked when I noticed he wasn't breathing. How I just ran and left him there, alone.

"I don't know what to do Darren. It's so fucked up. It was an accident."

I sit on the edge of his bed, my feet planted firmly on the floor. I drape one hand across my abdomen and rest my head in the other. I thought I would feel better after telling him, after asking for help. But I don't. I feel worse, more empty than before. I can feel the guilt starting to eat away at me already. I can feel myself starting to unravel even further. I don't know how I am going to live like this.

Darren sits on the bed beside me, puts his arm around me, stands up, sits back down, then jumps up.

"Okay," he says, running his hands through his hair.

"I'm going to fix this Beanie. Where are the clothes you were wearing when it happened?"

I stare at him for a minute, surprised at his sudden fervour.

"Dean, the clothes! Where are they?"

"Oh, er..." I shake my head, trying to get my thoughts right. "They're in the bin, in my room."

He wrenches the door of his wardrobe open, takes out an old schoolbag and rushes out of the room, leaving me sitting on the bed, confused. He returns a few seconds later. The bag is slung over his shoulder, looking far more full than it did coming out of the wardrobe.

"I'm going to get rid of these. You stay here. Don't go anywhere. Don't do anything."

"I won't," I say. "I don't even know what to do."

Darren looks at me, half smiles and walks out of the room, pulling the bag up tighter on his shoulder.

I walk back into my room, thinking about what Darren is doing now. For me. To protect me. But it won't matter. Nothing will matter anymore. I know exactly what I have to do. I have no other choice. Darren might be able to help with some suff, but he will never be able to help with the pain I am feeling. The guilt. It is tearing me apart. It will continue to tear me apart until there is nothing left. I cannot keep going on like this. I know that I will not survive. I will crumble, implode, go into a catatonic state from which there will be no escape.

So I know what I have to do.

I just have to.

But first I need to find Jimmy Browne.

CHAPTER THIRTY

The Request

I pull everything out of the drawer, throwing it onto the
floor until I find what I'm looking for. An old green and
orange, cammo *Action Man* wallet. Full of money, from
birthdays, from Easters, from every Christmas for as long
as I can remember. Every bit of money that I have ever
saved, have refrained from spending, in the hopes of one
day being able to put it to good use. And now it will be
used. Not for what I intended. But used nonetheless.

I take out a bundle of notes and place them in my back
pocket. That should be more than enough. I leave the rest
in the wallet and put it under the pillow on my bed. Mum
will find it there. It will help towards the costs. And, if I
know my mum, she will only want the best. But there's
no use thinking of that now. I don't bother picking everything up from the floor. I need to get out and back before
Darren returns, from wherever he is gone. I have to go find
Jimmy Browne.

◆ ◆ ◆

I stand in front of him with my hands stuffed in
my pockets, my eyes narrowed, my shoulders hunched,

adopting a somewhat submissive position so he knows I'm not here to attack him again. I have explained what I need but he hasn't said anything.

"Can you get it for me?" I ask him.

Jimmy looks at me with an expression on his face that I have never seen cross it before. I don't even know how to describe it. I can tell he hates me and I know I am taking a long shot here. But he is the only person I know that will be able to get me what I'm looking for.

"Why should I?"

"Can you get it for me?" I repeat, stepping closer to Jimmy, not in the mood for any games.

"Well...I could, but why should I, faggot?" He asks me, the corners of his mouth twitching, just itching to form a smile. "And what would you be wanting with one of them anyway?"

"That's none of your fucking business. I just need to know if you can get it."

Jimmy steps back and looks me up and down. He thinks he is so fucking smart. Thinks he is the fucking king of the crop. But he is fucking nothing. If I could put him in Jack's place I would do it in a fucking heartbeat. The world needs more Jacks and less Jimmy Brownes. The world needs-

"Okay, Turner, I'll get it for you. But it's gonna cost you and I doubt-"

He stops talking when he sees me pull the wad of cash out of my pocket. I hold it out to him and he hesitates for a second before reaching out and taking it into his own hand, splaying the notes wide in a fan-like shape.

"You're actually serious about this?"

"Yes, I'm fucking serious. Is it enough?" I gesture at the money in his hand and he counts it quickly, his thumb flicking through the worn notes, his tounge poking out at the corner of his mouth in concentration.

"Er, yeah, it will get you something small, probably used, but up to the job." He puts the cash into one of his trouser pockets and pulls his phone out of the other one. He cradles it in both hands, swiping and tapping quickly. He glances up at me. "If you gimme your number I'll text you later tonight when I have it and you can come collect it."

"No." I think for a minute as to where will be the best place for him to leave it for me. I can't take it home and I definitely do not want him texting me about it. He can drop it somewhere and I will pick it up. "You know the old distillery?" He nods. "There's a skip there. Leave it there, on the left hand side. I'll collect it from there. Just have it there by tomorrow morning."

He taps and swipes on his phone again, the silence growing between us.

"Alright," he says, after a minute. "Skip. Left hand side. By tomorrow morning. Done."

He puts his phone away and I start to turn, to walk away but he grabs me by the elbow. "I don't really give a shit what it is you're planning on doing, but you leave my name out of it, right!"

I stare at him for a moment, my lips pursed, trying not to show any emotion. I don't say anything, just nod my head slightly, pull my arm out of his grip and head home.

◆ ◆ ◆

I pick up everything that I threw onto the floor earlier and put it into the drawers, taking my time, arranging things neatly, making sure to fold the clothes properly and put them in order. I could just shove them in but I want to do it properly. I want my room to be tidy.

I check to make sure the wallet, with my savings, is still under the pillow where I left it. It is. I open it and count. There is a good amount. Mum will be able to use it well. I put it back under but leave it poking out at the corner, so it will be visible when someone comes in later. I grab my bag from the floor and pull out a notebook and a pen. I place them onto my desk, zip up the bag and leave it resting against the side of my wardrobe.

I close the door to my room gently, turn the lamp on top of my desk on, so that it illuminates the surface, where the pen and notebook are waiting for me. I take the pen into my hand, remove the lid and open the notepad to the first blank page I can find. I hesitate for a moment, thinking. I don't have to hand write these letters but I want to. I want to do it old school. It feels more personal. So they will know that what I write will be the truth.

I put the tip of the pen to the paper and write. This first letter I am writing is to my mum, to explain everything. To tell her about everything that has happened these past two weeks. I omit nothing. She deserves to know the truth. I tear the pages from the notebook and set them aside, turning to the next blank page. This one I am writing to Mrs. Hawkins. She also deserves to know everything. She needs to know that I am sorry for the hurt that I have caused her. My hand shakes as I write furiously, but I take a breath and steady it. I don't want it to become illegible. My eyes water but I hold back the tears. I need to focus on doing this. I tear these pages from the notebook too and set them down beside the others. I turn for the last time to another blank page and write. This time

I address my oldest and closest friend, Dave Rudden. I've been a shitty friend to him the past two weeks and he deserves to know why.

I finish writing and put the lid back on the pen, hold onto it, gathering up all the sheets of paper. The letters that will explain everything. The letters that will explain why I have to do what I am doing. I fold them over and put them into my pocket. I slip the notebook into the drawer nearest to me and head downstairs. I prise open the cupboard under the stairs, slowly, listening to my mum and dad chatting quietly in the living room, their voices drifting softly into my ears.

I feel around on the shelf in the cupboard until I find what I'm looking for. I take three envelopes out of the packet and head back up to my room. I sit at my desk, place each of the letters into each of the envelopes one by one, addressing them as I do. I lay them out in front of me and look at them, thinking...

I turn off the lamp and sit in darkness, waiting for morning to come, so that I can do what I have to do.

CHAPTER THIRTY- ONE

The End

Light floods in through the window of my room and I trun away from the desk, the letters gripped firmly in my hand. I walk over, stand by the door and look around, noticing the sheer banality of this room, compared to Jack's, how bland and beige it all is. I remember how Jack's room was an explosion of colour, coming at you from every direction, hitting you smack in the face. I never did get around to getting a purple lampshade either, never did get around to adding some character to my room, to getting some purple shadows of my own. Not that it even matters now. Nothing matters now.

I shove my cracked but still functioning phone into one of my pockets and put the letters into the other. I walk out onto the landing and stop when I hear a voice coming from Darren's room. I walk over to the door and listen carefully.

"Morning Jim, yeah I know it's early, sorry. It's just that I won't be able to come in today."

There's a pause and then Darren continues.

"No, I'm not sick, it's just a family situation."

Another pause.

"Great, thanks Jim and sorry again for the short notice, I'll make it up with a double shift next week."

I hear the springs of Darren's bed squeaking and I puff out my cheeks, suppressing a sigh. Another reason I have to do what I am about to do. I have landed Darren in it now and I shouldn't have. He shouldn't have to be shouldering my messed up situation.

I walk away from his door and plod gently down the stairs, glancing behind me as I head out, taking in the hallway, picturing the living room and kitchen in my mind, remembering what it was like in the mornings when my mum would be at the table, drinking her tea, at dinnertime when I would get home after school and we would all gather round the table, as a family, eating, chatting, telling each other about our days.

The air is cold on my face and hands as I walk down the driveway, past my dad's car and out onto the footpath. I count the steps as I walk, trying to keep my mind occupied, trying to keep it off the thought of what I am about to do.

I walk slowly into the main street in town and stop when I reach the post office, looking around me. It is still early so there aren't many people around and some of the shops still have their shutters down, not yet ready for today's business. But I am ready. To do what I have to do.

I slide the three envelopes from my pocket, feel the smooth paper against the skin of my hands. I raise them up and push them through the thin slot at the top of the post box. They drop in and I imagine they settle at the bottom, one on top of the other, waiting to be collected and delivered to their respective addressees.

I spot a quick movement out of the corner of my eye

and turn to look, the hairs on the back of my neck raising, getting a strange sensation that someone was just watching me. But there is nothing there. No one is walking past, the street ahead of me lies empty. A trick of the mind, maybe, my subconscious trying to deter me from doing what I have to do.

I stuff my hands into my pockets and walk away, heading now for the distillery. To see if Jimmy Browne has done what I have asked of him. If he has, then so be it. I will be able to do what I have to do. But if he hasn't I will need to act fast, get one from someone else. I'm sure it won't be too hard to find somebody with one in this shitty town.

I slip in through the gap in the fence and walk with determination, drawing level with the skip. I pull open the doors and scan the entire contents, seeing only rubble. I knew he wouldn't fucking do it. I should have known bett-

No wait. There. A piece of blue plastic sticking up at the left hand corner. I reach in, getting a grip on the plastic with the tips of my fingers. It is wedged in tightly so I have to pull hard until it comes loose. I stumble backwards as it pops out.

I hold the bag in my hands, feeling the shape of it through the thin plastic. I won't take it out. Not here in the open, where someone could see. I stuff it into the front of my trousers, pulling my top down over it, to conceal the noticeable bulge it is making on my abdomen. I make my way over to the door of the distillery. I remember the last time I prised my way inside the building and I do the same again, this time by myself, Jack not here to help me shift the large piece of wood away from the door. The wood comes away easily, being loose now, the nails, driven through the wood and into the concrete, no longer fixed permanently in their holes.

I bend and make for the hole that I busted in the door the other day, the plastic bag rubbing against my stomach as I get down on all fours and crawl through. I stand up and look around me, gazing at the large cylindrical vats around me, still glistening despite the layer of dust settled on top of them. I pull the plastic bag out of the waistband of my trousers, open it up and look at the contents within.

I take it out of the plastic bag, discarding that onto the floor and guage the weight of it in my hands. It is heavier than I expected. Heavier than they make them look in the movies. Not as shiny either. There are scuffs and scratches all over it. I wonder how many people have used it before me? A lot I expect. But I will probably be the last. Surely they will take it into evidence when they find it. Seal it up in one of those clear plastic bags with EVIDENCE written in big capital letters on the front. Send it off for analysis before it eventually gets locked up in a store room somewhere. Or does that just happen in movies and TV shows? I don't actually know. But it doesn't matter. I'm not going to find out now anyway.

I hold it in my left hand and let my arm fall gently to my side. Using my right hand I reach into in my pocket and take out my phone. I unlock it and go to the messaging app. I bring up my brother's name and type out a new message.

Meet me at the old distillery in town as soon as you can. Its important.

I read over the message several times and hit send, confident that it should be Darren to come get me. It would be too hard on anyone else, especially my mum. I feel my stomach tighten at the thought of this, the thought of her seeing me. It would destroy her. So, yes, it has to be my brother.

I place my phone back into my pocket and, transferring the gun to my right hand from my left, I raise it to my head, placing the tip of the barrel against my temple. The metal feels cold and hard on my skin, but I hold it in place, despite my shaking hand. I have to do this. I cannot live with myself any longer. I cannot live knowing what I have done. The pain I have caused. The hurt that is eating me up inside, the guilt, gnawing away at me, consuming me completely.

Sliding my finger in through the loop I rest it on the trigger. I picture Jack one last time. His beautiful smile, his soft warm skin. How happy we should have been. How I fucked everything up. For me. For him. For everyone.

As a tear falls from my my cheek to the dusty floor below, I hear a loud scraping come from behind me. My head starts to turn instinctively but I press the gun harder against my skull, quickly count to three, and squeeze the trigger.

The End...

...Kind of.

**Find Out What Happens Next
In Empty Colours: Book 2**

Yellow Mist

Coming Soon

www.dtmoorhousebooks.com

ACKNOWLEDGEMENT

I would like to take a moment to thank you, the reader. Firstly for choosing my book and secondly for sticking with it to the end. You could have chosen any number of books but you have chosen mine and have given it your time and attention. So for that and for you, I am eternally grateful.

It has always been a dream of mine to see a book with my name on it and to have as many people as possible read the stories that I have to tell. So now I have taken my first tentative steps in this venture and I would love to continue doing so for as long as I possibly can. But I can only do this with the help and support of readers. So I urge you to please spread the word, tell your friends, colleagues, family members about the new book you have read and have hopefully enjoyed. And if you have the time and would be so kind to do so, please leave a review on Amazon. It goes a long way towards helping self-published authors like myself.

Thank you,
D. T. Moorhouse

ABOUT THE AUTHOR

D. T. Moorhouse

D. T. Moorhouse is a Secondary School Teacher and now self-published author, from Ireland. He has a Bachelor of Arts in English and Linguistics and a Masters in Education from University College Dublin. He was born and raised in Crumlin, Dublin and now splits his time living between County Kildare and Dublin, in Ireland. Purple Shadows is his debut novel.

Contact And Find Out More About D. T. Moorhouse

Email: dtpmoorhouse@gmail.com

Website: www.dtmoorhousebooks.com

Facebook: www.facebook.com/dtpmoorhouse

Instagram: www.instagram.com/dtmoorhouse

Twitter: www.twitter.com/DTMoorhouse1

Printed in Great Britain
by Amazon

44521537R00131